THE CONTRACTED SOUL:

A TALE FROM THE MYST CITY CHRONICLES

LUKE ANTONY BAKER

Order this book online at www.trafford.com
or email orders@trafford.com

Most Trafford titles are also available at major online book retailers.

Printed in the United States of America.

ISBN: 978-1-4669-0866-6 (sc)
ISBN: 978-1-4669-0865-9 (hc)
ISBN: 978-1-4669-0867-3 (e)

Library of Congress Control Number: 2011962837

Trafford rev. 01/10/2012

 www.trafford.com

North America & international
toll-free: 1 888 232 4444 (USA & Canada)
phone: 250 383 6864 ♦ fax: 812 355 4082

PROLOGUE

T HE LAND OF TURBULUS is a land rich in history: the legends
of the founders, the wars that sha1ped the land, and various
ancient curiosities. These stories and others are buried in the
archives of the greatest wizards and historians in the land. The
royal library in Myst City is the richest of these.

This is a story of sorcery, war, betrayal, chaos, destiny, and a
great journey in the darkest of times.

Our prelude begins with the formation of the Grand Alliance.
The armies of Sunrise City, Myst City, Darkwoods Outpost and
Plateau City were the sworn defenders of the Capital, home of the
royal family. This union of the land's greatest powers was a result
of the great threat from the forces of darkness.

There existed a great evil in the lands, Zuul, the demon
considered the overture of an apocalypse. She waged a savage war
raged across the land for decades. Massacres and savagery claimed
countless souls.

Zuul was searching for those chosen by destiny to be the mystic keys. These keys were powerful sorcerers. They were five in number. Once the souls of these five keys were assembled in the Temple of Destiny, they could open The Arcane Gate, the entrance to the sacred altar, a hallowed temple said to house the powers of the gods. This altar would bestow upon the one who asked a wish of whatever he or she desired.

The gate had been closed eons ago by the combined power of the gods, and only prophets could open it. The Temple of Destiny eventually fell under Zuul's control and became known as the Temple of the Damned.

With her almighty power she created the seven demon lords. They were the demonic embodiment of man's greatest sins, culled from the underworld itself. With these demons she assembled an army to conquer Turbulus.

Towns were razed, peoples massacred, and the land itself was dying. The Grand Alliance suffered one massive defeat after the other until they made their stand on The Great Fields; however for reasons unknown Darkwoods Outpost had deserted the Grand Alliance in its hour of need. The second-in-command to Zuul, Wrath; the embodiment of anger and hatred stood firm as General of Zuul's armies.

Zuul herself sat on her throne on the cliffs above the battle to watch it unfold. She reveled in the suffering of others and quenched her sadistic nature during what would later be known as the Twilight Wars. She relished the day she would open the Arcane Gate and gain infinite power and immortality.

The armies of the Grand Alliance had discovered the identities of the keys to the Arcane Gate—the ancient prophets' latest incarnations and had hidden them in safety. Zuul, infuriated, had waged a genocidal war against the Grand Alliance vowing not to stop until they surrendered the sages to her.

What began as a skirmish on the Great Plains had escalated far beyond what either side had expected; all armies were assembled on these fields for what would be the final battle to decide the fate of Turbulus. Wrath and the other six demonic embodiments stood on one side with their grotesque legions and the Grand Alliance stood on the other.

The snarling beasts and abominations of Zuul's army would have terrified even the bravest of men. The hulking ogres, trolls and golems stood on one side, surrounded by goblins, zombies, and the other beasts, all of them Zuul's recruits.

The other side, humans, elves, and dark elves stood in formation willing to defend the land with their very lives. Their matching bronze armor and weapons readied, they stood in formation beneath the banners of their three armies. Almost to signal the start of battle, a mighty storm gathered overhead, a torrent of rain soon followed. The Grand Commander of the Alliance, Laru stood at the forefront. With paired horn blasts from Wrath and Laru, the battle began.

Laru, was the mightiest soldier the Grand Alliance had at their disposal. Even though he was secretly the prophet of light, he refused to be hidden away from Zuul and chose to confront her as the Commander of the Grand Alliance.

The bloody battle raged on for hours, neither side yielding. The sorcerers of the Grand Alliance had sealed away in stone the Demon Lords, all but two of the demonic tyrants—Wrath and Zuul, the most powerful. Seeing the battle unfolding and the Grand Alliance gaining control, Zuul stepped into the fray.

Her hulking form clad in the darkest of armor, she stomped slowly through the battle, the conflict stopping to a hush as she walked.

The lines of soldiers of the Grand Alliance swarmed Zuul; only to be knocked back effortlessly with powerful black magic, vaporized. Zuul, holding a deathly blade above her head cast a tremendous summoning spell on the soldiers, their charred remains rose to serve her as mindless zombies.

The sorcerers of the Grand Alliance once again stepped in, they failed to seal Zuul; she was far too strong. With the enchanted relic, the Spear of Destiny, rumored to kill even demons, a paladin, took her by surprise, impaling her spine, before being knocked back with a fatal blow. Taking advantage of this opportunity, Laru with his holy sword cast a mighty magical array around the beast.

The length of the spear was buried in her tainted gut. Foul, black blood streamed down the length of the weapon as Zuul twisted and tugged the piercing spike. Zuul, after relentless struggling managed to snap the spearhead off to remove the pole. She lay helpless under the containment spell around her.

The demon crackled and shook, seeing their opportunity to seal her; the sorcerers of the Grand Alliance opened Pandora's Box, a powerful relic of confinement. However, Zuul's power was too great to be contained, so Laru siphoned it to be contained in a trusted guardian. Now weakened by this spell, Pandora's Box could then contain the beast's spirit; her immortal body was banished to the pit.

It is said that Zuul still remains chained up in the pits of the underworld, awaiting her release to continue her unholy campaign for infinite power.

The battle tapered off after that, the demon lord Wrath retreated with his dwindling army to the Temple of the Damned. Zuul's armies had been defeated. Pandora's Box was entrusted to the Grand Inquisitor, an ancient wizard, who concealed it somewhere in Turbulus.

For a while there was peace, until Wrath, the surviving demon lord revived his brethren from their prison as statues, restoring their life. However, their faith in Zuul was broken, and their powers only a fraction of what they once were. They remained divided, squabbling over leadership, awaiting Zuul's return.

The demon lords still conquered territories separately, but they weren't as strong as before when united under Zuul. Wrath assumed Zuul's role as leader and a few of the demons followed him, inspired by their own selfish goals, though many of them remained divided.

Upon learning of Pandora's Box, Wrath set out to find it. Once he heard the legend of Zuul's great power being contained in the guardian's bloodline, he scoured the land to discover them. If he could do so, he could restore his mistress' power once she was reborn.

The Grand Inquisitor kept Pandora's Box hidden from everyone, concealing it away forever.

For over a century Wrath searched, waiting for the chance to revive his mistress. As his campaign failed, life in Turbulus returned to something approaching peace. As the centuries passed, Wrath was beginning to lose hope he would ever revive Zuul and could only wait for one of the guardian's bloodline to be discovered

ONE

CRACK! A STICK BROKE as the deer sped through the tangled thicket of twisted, bare trees in Heartless Swamp. The green mist that clung to the trees gave off a foul stench as if from a sewer.

Lady Crow, a sorceress of the dark arts, resided in her run-down cabin tucked away in this gloomy cesspool. She had instructed her two pupils to seek out and catch a deer for dinner without weapons.

This may be an impossible task for most, but these two boys were apprentices of the dark arts and had an arsenal of tricks up their sleeves.

The two apprentices, Umbra and Micah, sped after the deer; they evaded claw-like branches and dodged roots with great skill. The air was heavy and humid. Their black cloaks flowed behind them like dark shadows; they were gaining on their prey as it rustled through the brush.

On top of being apprentices to Lady Crow, Umbra and Micah were also rivals. Today's exercise was no different from the other grueling competitions they were often assigned. Only the one able to catch the speeding deer was granted dinner with their teacher; the loser would be forced sit in silence and watch them consume the meal to motivate them the next day's challenge; feeding only on the scraps.

Umbra, easily the more gifted of the two was almost within arm's reach of the deer. Micah was nearly neck and neck with him as they locked onto their quarry.

"Ahh!" Micah yelped as he caught a sharpened tree branch, which carved straight through his cheek. Eyes scrunched in pain, he did not see the massive wall of a tree and ran smack into it with a loud, wet thump.

Umbra, not realizing and completely focused on his target reached into his cloak pocket to extract a small glass vial filled with goat blood. He popped the cap and then dipped his finger into the blood-filled vial, swirling it around thoroughly before removing it.

Using his bloodied finger he sketched a small circular symbol on the palm of his hand. He stamped his hand on his forehead and began to whisper an incantation under his breath. All the while he maintained his pursuit, dodging the winding thicket effortlessly.

He stopped dead in his tracks, kicking up mud, and quickly smacked his palm on the nearest tree. The markings on his forehead lit up in glowing crimson, illuminating the damp wood around him. Suddenly the swamp floor began to rumble under his feet; instantly a sharp spear of a tree root shot up from the moist earth and pierced cleanly through the deer's neck!

The deer frozen in horror, dropped lifelessly to the ground as the root dissolved. Micah returned to the fray only to witness his defeat.

"Damn! You win again Umbra," Micah moaned smacking his fist on the nearest slime-caked tree as he bent over to catch his breath. Umbra turned to face him with a cheeky smile on his face, the symbol on his forehead fading away to nothing. The two apprentices were hunched over now as they caught their breath. Micah wiped his bleeding cheek.

"You're still sneaking me some of that food, right?" he inquired turning his head to Umbra with a mischievous grin.

"Of course, you would have starved to death long ago if I hadn't been," Umbra jested, returning the smile. The two groaned as they dragged the limp carcass back through the mud, lifting it over the shrubs and down the arduous trail towards Lady Crow's house.

The walk was long, through swampy ground plagued with dead, twisted trees. The stench of the green fog no longer bothered the two apprentices since they had spent over a year in this swamp.

It was a wonder how anything even lived in this hellhole, every step your foot would sink in the muck, every time you passed a tree you would snag yourself on a sharp branch. The land itself seemed to stew in perpetual despair.

"So how do you think we'll eat this deer?" Micah inquired with a grunt, as they stumbled southerly across through wetland towards the house.

There was an evil set of yellow eyes glaring menacingly from the nearby marsh. The creature raised its head out of the water to reveal a vine-entangled, slime covered figure—a mire beast! A grotesque combination of hulking ogre, tangled vines and muck, the mire beast raised its filthy head out of the marsh and stared hungrily at the two young necromancers.

"Crap!" shrieked Micah. The two ragged and exhausted apprentices gawked at each other, exchanging expressions of terror.

"We can't come back empty-handed! This thing isn't taking our deer!" Micah asserted, masking his fatigue. The two of them dropped their prize and stood back-to-back in a defensive stance as the mire beast stepped out onto the banks of the marsh and shambled closer to them.

The entangled vines covering the beast pulsed like veins, muck dripping as it moved. The two apprentices saw spattered blood around the creature's lips and knew it had just fed.

"Have any ideas?" Umbra whispered to Micah.

"Just follow my lead!" Micah replied, reaching deep into his pockets to extract a small sachet of salt. Umbra in turn did the same. "Flash, bang and then we run for it!"

A simple enough spell, it would momentarily blind the beast. They could then grab the deer and flee. Micah and Umbra nodded to each other. They poured themselves a small handful of salt from a sachet they kept handy and began whispering identical chants under their breath. The salt lit up in their hands as they prepared to pelt the mire beast.

"Take that!" yelled Umbra, as he and Micah tossed the salt. The salt popped loudly on contact with the beast's slimy, root-tangled body as a thick white smoke veiled its head.

"Run!" Umbra cried out as he and Micah each grabbed an end of the deer and raised the animal above their heads. Adrenaline kicking in once more, they fled towards the trees. After only a few feet, Micah lost his boot in the mud, tumbling over. Umbra, too stumbled, dropping the deer. Closing in behind them was an extremely aggravated mire beast!

Seeing no chance to run, Umbra called upon his dark powers, hurling a bolt of shadow magic at his aggressor. The bolt knocked the creature off balance just as it was within reach of Micah with its muddy, clawed hands. Micah frantically continued pulling his foot free as Umbra kept the beast's attention.

As the beast inched closer, its forehead singed from Umbra's last attack, the apprentice looked around frantically for a way to topple this adversary. That's when he saw the deer they had been carrying. He closed his eyes, focusing his power for a moment, casting a black stream of magic towards the dead deer, surrounding it. Umbra swung his hand in a whipping motion; the deer's bones were pulled from its body and flung as sharpened projectiles at the mire beast.

The mire beast froze for a moment, hundreds of bone fragments piercing its body, before collapsing lifelessly into the swamp.

"Umbra, you saved me. Again," Micah panted, having finally freed his foot from the muck.

"I think I ruined the deer though," Umbra groaned. The carcass was shredded to pieces. "Unless . . ." Umbra continued thoughtfully.

"No, Umbra, we can't eat the mire beast, now that's just disgusting!" Micah interjected.

"I guess we can make deer soup," Umbra snickered.

Micah laughed as they gathered up the pieces and continued home.

"She is going to chew us out over this," Umbra sighed. He and Lady Crow were always arguing, Micah wondered what kept them from killing each other sometimes.

"Sure she's tough as nails and a self-centered troll, but she is a good teacher, I feel stronger and faster every day thanks to her training," Micah assured him. "It will be worth it in the end when I can leave here as a great sorcerer." He added, looking thoughtfully to the clouded sky as he spoke.

He had always been the softer, more understanding of the two and always kept Umbra's bad temper in check. Their motivations were very different: Umbra's for power to help serve his own personal needs; and Micah's was power to help others. Despite their contrary personalities, they got along very well.

The air was thick with fog as the two apprentices shuffled home, caked in mud. They were fully aware of why Lady Crow lived out here—she was banished from her old village for necromancy, she didn't bother to conceal it either. Her house was littered with necromantic tomes and books of divination.

Umbra had taught himself the tree root spell after pursuing dinner, day in day out. Micah would rarely win in these contests but he was sure to rub it in Umbra's face when he did. They were not just rivals, they were friends as well.

At the end of the trail ahead the house became visible, or rather the dilapidated shack, which sat across from a monument to a long-forgotten war.

The war was ancient, so the monument and its cemetery were abandoned to history books, swallowed up by the contagion of the swamp. This was perfect of course, for Lady Crow's brand of magic. With all her necromancy spells over the years she had probably unearthed enough skeleton minions with her dark magic to have emptied the cemetery. The overturned soil from the plots was proof enough of this.

These minions would serve their purpose for an hour or so then crumble as the magic faded, leaving a pile of dust for Umbra and Micah to sweep up. When they were animate though, they were terrifying to behold. Their glowing eye-sockets, pulsing browned bones and stiff movement would terrify any who saw it.

Umbra and Micah were used to seeing these animate skeletons around from time to time; they were even capable of reviving one or two at a time with necromancy. It was a simple ritual, a blood circle; some candles, an incantation and the dead would rise as slaves to the practitioner. Lady Crow's prowess in this art meant she did not require a ritual to revive them. With her black gem bracelet and a moment of concentration she could unearth dozens at once.

As the wreck of a house emerged through the fog, Micah and Umbra decided to let Umbra's root trick be kept secret. Lady Crow would scorn them for using other schools of magic saying: "You came here to learn necromancy! Don't waste your efforts on those pointless childish tricks!" The last thing they needed after this exhausting chase was a lecture.

They stepped onto the squeaking step of the battered, old, wooden porch only to see a rat scurry away. The candle-lit house was welcome only in the sense it was slightly warmer than outside. As they crossed the threshold they were acknowledged by Lady Crow with a stern look, she shook her head with a deep sigh when she saw the shredded carcass.

"What took you so long? You were gone for a whole hour!" she complained. Umbra held back his frustration with a reassuring glance from Micah.

Lady Crow stood there—a wrinkled old woman leaning on her twisted, old bone cane. She always wore a tattered old dark dress and a purple shawl over her shoulders.

She expected her two students to wear black necromancer robes when in her presence. The robes were uncomfortable and did not fit the boys but they got used to them. They would chuckle to themselves about how they looked like undertakers.

Lady Crow pointed to the kitchen and sat down on the squeaky old couch and watched the smoldering brick fireplace. Her wrinkled face illuminated by the crackling fire was eerie to say the least.

"Umbra won again I presume?" she predicted not even turning to face her students. Umbra caught a glimpse of sadness on Micah's face from Lady Crow's assumption. She had come to expect Umbra winning. She sat down on her old dusty couch in the dimly-lit room. Peeling navy-trimmed wallpaper hung on the old plaster walls and the occasional framed picture of Lady Crow in her youth dotted the room.

It was curious, she would often make Umbra and Micah clean the house, but within an hour it would be right back to its original spooky state. The house seemed to resent being cleaned and would dirty itself. She eventually stopped asking them to do it and simply ignored the conditions.

"Micah, you cook that deer in a stew and Umbra, you sit," she ordered. The two students obediently complied. Micah dragged the carcass past the kitchen to the pantry to butcher it being careful not to mess up the carpet. Umbra wondered why be bothered, the carpet was a mess anyway. "Don't expect dinner to be ready soon," Lady Crow continued in her miserable tone.

Umbra, although hungry was used to waiting long periods to eat. "So how did you catch that deer?" she inquired, turning around to eye Umbra suspiciously.

"Well, we didn't use weapons. It was more a collaborative effort. Micah cornered it and I dealt the finishing shot with a blood shard." He was referring to a favored spell by Lady Crow where a small droplet of blood was magically hardened into a sharpened projectile and cast at the victim. Lady Crow's suspicious expression remained.

"Show me your blood vial," she demanded stretching out her wrinkled old hand. Umbra handed it over and watched her roll it around in her grip. Sure enough, the vial wasn't full. She tossed it back at him satisfied with his story. She stared into the fireplace once more. "I hope that fool hasn't wasted the valuable parts of that deer."

"Micah does try, you never acknowledge it though!" Umbra snapped at the bitter old witch.

"When he does something worth acknowledging, I will! Go and clean up for dinner!"

Two

THAT NIGHT UMBRA AND Micah slept on the dusty old couches. A rusted chandelier hung loosely, swaying in the wind by the open window. The noises outside were soothing, if not a little creepy. Umbra stared at the gentle swaying of the chandelier as he drifted off to sleep.

A familiar nightmare crept into Umbra's head. One he had suffered from for years now and vivid enough to feel real. It was his childhood memories of tragedy and isolation. It was the very reason he traveled out to this swampy wasteland to learn magic from a miserable, old witch.

The images were as clear as ever. Umbra was once again walking through the woods carrying a basket of apples he had gathered from a nearby orchard.

It was peaceful back then, the autumn breeze bringing its sweet aroma of flowers into his nostrils. The crisp apples still beaded with dew as he carried them in a small thatched basket. The sun was dipping over the horizon as he strode carefree through the pine woods, oblivious to the world.

His mind always pondered the same question when he was alone.

Where had Father gone to?

It had been a whole year since his father had up and left.

He remembered it vividly; rain was storming, lashing with unusual ferocity. The dripping gaps in their roof had woken him. He awoke only to see his father don a beige trench-coat and flat-cap, and march out the door. His steps were heavy like he was carrying a great burden. Breaking eye contact with Umbra in a saddened gaze he had disappeared forever.

It wasn't a feeling of anger that swept over Umbra, but a nostalgic feeling of uneasiness. His father seemed to be running away from something, but Umbra couldn't tell what it was.

His fonder memories were of his father, teaching him some sorcery as a child, watching him proudly with his illuminated smile as Umbra grew more adept. He began with simple tricks: reviving small flowers, shooting down apples with magical darts, stirring tea with levitating spoons, creating small snacks for food. They were all charming little spells he used to impress his friend Marin with.

He had a crush on her as far back as he could remember, and thinking of her always brought a smile to his face. They had been friends forever and he was too shy to tell her how he felt. He still held dear her playful laugh and flowing blonde hair. He loved her and still did.

He was content with the simple magic for a while, but one of his father's books had always caught his eye. Grimoire of the Damned, it was named, a book on necromancy. Umbra was sure there were others, but he hadn't gone into his father's study since the night he had walked out. There was still dust on the brass doorknob to the study door. His father had always scorned him for looking at his more 'occult' tomes. This had only inflated his curiosity further.

His mother cried endlessly when his father left, she wouldn't get out of bed for days on end and would break into hysterical crying when his name was mentioned.

"No Umbra, father isn't coming home," she would say tearfully whenever he asked.

She finally came to terms with it after crying a river of tears for him.

Life for them continued on after that. His mother ignored the gossip circulating around their small town of Brie and lived life as though nothing had happened.

She would always wear a smile and that red dress was her favorite. She kept her dark, flowing hair tied up.

Umbra had inherited that dark hair, but he kept it short. Although recently under orders from his teacher he had grown a braid to signify his apprenticeship; For the most part things in Brie were happy.

Rumors of strange happenings going on outside the town began to circulate. Stories of children disappearing in the middle of the night and whole cities set ablaze, but that world seemed far away to the simple folk living in the lush foothills of this small hamlet. It was, to them, another world separate from their own.

It was a typical early evening. The night-washed sky was setting in and Umbra had left to gather some fruit for dessert. He had enjoyed a great hearty dinner and stepped outside with a beaming smile on his face.

The sun was just setting when he stepped out of the modest little cottage. The straw-thatched roof rustled in the wind and the shadows danced on the bricks as he strode off towards the orchard on the other side of the woods.

However, something tainted was in the air today; Umbra couldn't quite put his finger on it. It was subtle but sent a chill down his spine. Uneasy, Umbra set off to gather apples, unable to shake that feeling.

About half way back from the woods, Umbra heard screaming from the direction of the town. He looked ahead curiously to see smoke rising. Glinted with embers, flames raced towards the evening sky, their tips licking like serpents' tongues on the heavens. The houses ignited one after the other; the town was awash in an eerie glow.

Citizens were running in every direction screaming, terrifying dark-cloaked figures chasing them, not running, but gliding. The figures were taller than the people; they wielded dull swords and axes. Their shriveled grey hands clutched their weapons as they sliced mercilessly through everyone in their path.

Umbra could only look on in horror from the edge of the darkened forest as these monsters cut down the men, women, and children he had known his whole life. Their screams echoing in the night sky as their worlds were torn down.

After a few minutes, the figures assembled in the town square forming a circle. The darkened figure of a sorcerer stood in the center and cast a spell array, lighting up the square with a purple eerie glow. The figures vanished suddenly into a black haze, leaving the devastation of their brutal killing spree and the flaming houses in their wake.

As Umbra gathered his courage, he bolted down the shallow hill towards his mother's cottage. The devastation, the screaming, crying, fire, and smell of death seemed distant to him as he raced towards his destination.

He barely got into view of his house when he saw a bloodied figure lying face-down on the ground. Dark hair was flowing in the wind and a hand was outstretched, frozen in a gesture of desperation. His mother lay lifeless and bloodied in front of him, a dagger in her side. Umbra could only look on in horror as tears poured down his face and he broke down.

Nearly half the town was taken that night, it became known as the Night of Flames. A memorial was placed in the town cemetery behind the chapel to serve as a constant reminder. The attackers' identities still remained unknown to the citizens. They had never seen creatures such as these before—skeletal and withered, armed with weapons and gliding silently as they moved.

Town meetings were called for ideas on how to defend against another attack, but after realizing the futility of any defense they could muster they simply prayed it never reoccur.

Umbra stood alone in his empty house, it was silent and every room was full of memories that now seemed like distant past to him. Everything reminded him of his mother, her perfume still lingered all around the house.

He couldn't stand the pain of being alone anymore; he raced up the stairs to his father's study, kicking open the door and browsing his bookshelf.

He found exactly what he was looking for: Grimoire of the Damned—the solution to all of his problems. He remained isolated by himself in intense study, feeding only on conjured snacks as he scoured the tome for a solution.

THREE

T HE MONTHS FLEW BY, and the town returned to its normal, peaceful state. The townsfolk had left the empty houses untouched to serve as memorials to those lost families, occasionally leaving flowers on their doorsteps. The townspeople assumed Umbra was a victim of that massacre and were unaware of his absence as he stowed himself away in his father's study, books open everywhere.

Umbra studied relentlessly from the grimoire and the other books on the dark arts he had found in his father's collection. Until, at last, he had stumbled across a ritual—a revival ritual.

Umbra knew that in a town as religious as Brie, what he was planning was a criminal act. Necromancy was a condemned school of magic, but he was desperate.

He knew that if he went through with his plan to resurrect his mother and was discovered, he would be condemned as a heretic and hated by all of his neighbors. If he could succeed, and concoct a believable yarn to conceal his actions he would have his mother and normal life back. He continued to indulge in that fantasy as he studied tirelessly the rituals of demonology, a magical school detested by the populace even more than necromancy.

He reminisced of his mother waiting on the porch for him to return with a basket of fruit, welcoming him with a loving smile and open arms.

He had to do it!

As a few months passed and he was confident of his abilities he decided he was finally ready.

The moon was full and the town darkened. As the village snoozed, Umbra crept from his house. He carried with him a small brown sack and a shovel. He knew what he had to do, and he was determined to follow through with his plan. His mother would be alive again and life would return to the way it was.

Down the darkened alleys he crept, careful to not make any noise. When he finally reached the cemetery, storm clouds began to gather. Swinging open the old iron gates, he winced at the squeaky noise they made.

He scanned the gravestones, finding his mother's plot immediately. A weeping willow hung over the grave, sighing in the wind as he gathered himself. His memorial lay next to it, and he glanced at the empty plot and wondered why they had buried an empty coffin. A bead of sweat ran down his forehead as he returned to his mother's grave and stuck the shovel into the soft earth to begin digging.

The moon hung over the cemetery, peeping curiously between the clouds, the night was as quiet as a hushed child. Only the sounds were of dirt turning out of a growing hole and the rustling willow tree. Umbra ignored the worms, the mud on his clothes, his blisters from the shovel, and the rising damp chill he felt. He dug tirelessly until he finally struck the wood of his mother's coffin.

He rummaged through his bag until his hand felt the cold iron of a crowbar.

In one swift movement he unhinged the coffin's lid and peered under it. The smell! It was overpowering, he wasn't expecting it to be so pungent. He covered his nose, and gagged. All he had to do now was sketch a circle around the grave and begin the ritual. He shambled out of the grave with his nose pinched.

Hovering over the grave like a ghoul, he opened the grimoire and began reading. Following the tome's instructions, he drew a circular array with piece of chalk. Once the circle was drawn and lit candles had been placed strategically on the array he formed, it was ready.

Next the ritual called for a few drops of his blood. He looked nervously at the glimmering dagger tucked under his belt. Putting the book down and placing a small iron goblet at his feet he unsheathed the small dagger and held it reluctantly over his palm.

He took a deep breath and reminded himself that it was for his mother, flinching as he dragged the cold steel across his quivering hand. He held the dripping wound over the small goblet and continued to read, glancing down. Next he tossed the goblet into the pit. As the blood spilled in, the array lit up fiercely in the darkest crimson. The moon too, began to match its ferocity as his surroundings blurred and churned like he was in the eye of a storm.

The air around Umbra grew thick, warm, almost like breath. The smell of rot was replaced by the smell of sulfur.

A hulking figure rose up from the grave and swirled in a cloud of red, finally condensing, forming a glowing red demon, illuminated further by the raging light of the array. He had called forth the contract demon, Belphagor.

The demon's arms were crossed and his red wings were outstretched, muscles covered his body. He was a terrifying sight to behold. Umbra, taken back by it fell onto his rear. The demon's glassy eyes scanned Umbra up and down and with unmoving lips a growling voice boomed: "You have summoned me, mortal! What do you want?" The smell of sulfur from Belphagor's breath was nauseating.

"Restore this woman to life and vitality, this is all I ask of you," Umbra piped up, nervousness stricken in his voice. The bargaining had begun. "What do you want in return?" Umbra inquired with a gulp.

"I know exactly what I want from you, boy!" the demon chuckled. "You have three years and then your soul belongs to me!" the demon demanded.

"Three years! I'm not agreeing to that!" Umbra shot back at the demon, his fear had been replaced by frustration, though he was still hesitant to step forward.

Belphagor's eyes narrowed into a harsh glare. "Then surely you won't mind if I burn this corpse, it's stinking up the place, I'd be doing you a huge favor," the demon pointed down at the exposed corpse of Umbra's mother as his finger lit up in flame.

"No! Wait! I'll agree, just don't do it!" Umbra pleaded in desperation. The demon eyed him up and down, relinquished his finger of fire and stepped towards him; each step rotted the grass beneath his feet.

"You have three years! Then I will return to claim my prize, your soul. Here's a small reminder," the demon's eyes glowed and Umbra's hand burst into fire.

"Aaaaaargh!" Umbra screamed as he rolled around on the damp grass trying to put it out. The fire faded to a glowing ember, leaving a strange scar on the back of his hand. A symbol had been burnt into it.

Before Umbra could ask what it was, the demon was gone.

Still clutching his smoldering hand, Umbra peered into the grave which was now filled with smoke. Something was moving under the smoke!

"Mother!" Umbra called out like an expectant child no longer caring who heard him. His scar still glowed like a burning ember.

A hand emerged, but there was something seriously wrong, Umbra's expectant smile faded.

The hand was still withered and rotting! Next the head emerged; lifeless glassy eyes stared back at him. The corpse had only been animated into a mindless monster!

This creature that resembled his mother climbed out of the pit and crawling towards him now, its bones cracking, bile spewing as it moved. The foul smell had worsened and the twisted, grotesque figure terrified Umbra, paralyzing him with fear, his eyes laden with tears.

"Sssssssssssssssssssssssssssssssssssson" it gurgled. Then it let erupted with a bone-chilling shriek that echoed around the town. Umbra dropped to his knees covering his ears as the sound rang out. The noise was deafening!

Lights flickered on as candles were lit in the houses around him. Talking was heard and doors burst open revealing horrified villagers.

Before long, villagers were outside with lanterns and axes. The smoke still rising from the cemetery, clouding over the moon, it was obvious where the sound originated from.

They formed a mob as they marched; the cemetery was lit up like daylight by all the searing torches. Condemning yells with angry faces, and pitchforks waved as the mob grew in size, barely squeezing through the old iron gates.

The villagers saw Umbra with the figure surrounded by the ritual arrays and quickly realized what had transpired.

"Explain yourself; boy!" demanded the mayor, standing at the front of the pack, still in his bed-clothes.

Umbra was lost for words as he stared back at the mayor with terrified eyes.

"Monster!"

"Heretic!"

Accusations filled the air from the angry citizens.

They swarmed Umbra, holding him down as others hacked up the shambling monster with their axes, blood showering on the mob. They turned their attention to him, and he was lifted above the crowd. They were now carrying him towards the hills.

Wait a second! That's where they hang criminals! Umbra realized.

Umbra screamed and pleaded as he kicked and struggled in vain, but his pleas fell on deaf ears. The swarming mass of angry villagers yelled condemnations and threats as they carried Umbra up the hill. The dark landscape lit up around them as they marched; the roaring fire of their torches was matched only by their burning fury.

The world around him blurred, his head spun and the smell of rot still clung to his simple, grey clothes. Luckily for Umbra, a small glass vial of blood remained unnoticed in his pocket as the mob carried him to the gallows atop the hill.

The old wooden gallows stood at the edge of the woods, blood-stained ropes hung there, swaying in the gathering winds. Rain was pouring down now, the sky clouded and thunder cracked.

The mob's roars and chants filled the air around. *I'm done for!* Umbra thought to himself as his hands were bound behind him and he was placed in the noose.

The Contracted Soul

Just before they pulled the lever to release the trap door beneath his feet to let him hang, he uncapped the vial in his back pocket. He furiously scribbled a symbol on his back under his shirt with a bloodied finger. His face went pale and his body went limp. He had died there, condemned as a heretic.

A day later he awoke in the woods, he had been dumped there in a reeking ditch with the corpses of criminals.

The ground was soft and squishy, but it wasn't soil. Umbra's stomach turned as he clawed his way up the muddy hill out of the corpse pit, the worms writhed under his fingers. A severed noose still hung around his neck.

His escape plan had worked: resulting in temporary death! He technically was dead, killed by his own magic but only for twenty-four hours. During that time he had been as cold as ice and pale as snow. It was one of the simpler spells he had found in his dad's occult books.

He lay there on the wet ground, covered with dead leaves and smelling of rot. He began playing over the events in his head, barely believing how badly things had gone wrong. He lay there in the middle of the forest looking up at the night sky. A grim realization dawned on him: he had nobody.

Umbra awoke covered in a cold sweat to the familiar, dank surroundings of Lady Crow's shack.

The familiar iron chandelier swayed in the light breeze while the noises of the swamp still chirped predictably. At least here he had Micah as company. He rolled over to see Micah sleeping soundly on the other dusty couch, and decided not to wake him.

FOUR

UMBRA LAY SILENTLY IN the darkened room staring at the unlit lantern on the table. Just as he was drifting off back to sleep, sounds of growls erupted from Lady Crow's room down the hall. The first startling him, the noises grew louder.

Umbra sat up and listening carefully to the muffled noises, barely making out making out what was being said.

"No! You can't. I won't! Hissssssssssss, I will, you can't hold me forever! I will be free again!" echoed from down the hall.

Micah was a heavy sleeper and didn't even flinch, and remained sleeping silently on the other dusty couch across the room from Umbra. *Was there another person in Lady Crow's room?* Umbra wondered as his curiosity grew.

"Hisssssssssssssssssssssssss!" echoed a cry from down the hall, the walls seemed to shake and the house pulsed.

Umbra climbed to his feet, pulled on his grey tunic and lit a nearby lantern with a simple spark spell by clicking his fingers. The room glowed dimly under the light as Umbra crept out into the hall, careful not to tread on the creaking floorboards.

"No! I won't . . . You can't!" echoed Lady Crow's voice from down the hallway.

Umbra crept down the narrow hallway lined with peeling navy wallpaper. Dotted pictures of a family resembling Lady Crow hung on the wall in old wooden frames. She had never mentioned having a family, let alone any specific details of her exile to this swampy shack.

When Umbra had asked her about it she would snap at him and assign him a difficult task.

Still, Umbra crept until he got to the bleached wooden door at the end of the hallway, carefully pressing it open a crack to peer into Lady Crow's bedroom.

There she was, kicking, and groaning in her sleep under her navy bed-sheets. Umbra held up the lantern, shining a slim beam of light into the room.

There was something wrong!

Lady Crow's eyes were wide open, yet she was undoubtedly asleep, even stranger there were no pupils, only solid white in her eyes!

Umbra stepped back into the hallway and stood quietly for a few moments trying to make sense of it all.

The noise had died down now and Umbra figured it was just her having a bad nightmare. But, he had to be sure. He pushed the door open just enough to slip into the room.

Surely she would have something about this in her books. He looked over to the modest shelf opposite her bed. He crept carefully across the hardwood floors, being sure not to make noise, his lantern turned down almost all the way.

He finally got to the shelf. The books were dusty, just like everything else in this house, but one wasn't. It had been recently moved.

How strange! He thought as he slipped it out of the shelf and examined it under his lantern: Grimoire Demonus it read, it was a small leather-bound book with a lock, but the lock was open!

He opened it to the first page and instantly recognized the nature of the book. It was a book on demonology! Even stranger—it had a bookmark in it!

Umbra flicked carefully over to that section. *Exorcism rituals!* Under that passage was one on astral projection into dreams of a sleeper.

Perfect! I can see her dreams and try to figure out what's going on here.

He read through it carefully. It required a rare herb. Luckily he had seen this herb growing in the swamp: Dragon's bane, a small thorny plant as red as blood. It also required salt and blood, simple enough! He carried salt on him and Lady Crow gave them animal blood in vials to use for spells.

So he decided that the next night he would check to see what was going on inside Lady Crow's head!

"What are you doing!?" yelled a voice, it was Lady Crow! Umbra spun around, concealing the grimoire under his shirt. "Well boy, you better have a good explanation to be sneaking around my room late at night!" she barked. She was furious as she climbed out of bed to her feet.

Umbra couldn't get over how grotesquely old she was, it was enhanced by the dim lantern's light.

"I uh, wanted um . . ." Umbra looked around to see a small blanket curled up in the corner. "A blanket! I was cold you see and . . ." he lied.

"Get back to bed!" Lady Crow ordered almost at the volume of a scream. "Tomorrow you will be collecting fire-wood, alone!" she barked, pointing out the door. Umbra hung his head and walked back into the hallway and towards the couch carrying his lantern. Lady Crow slammed the door behind him.

Umbra tossed and turned on the couch. Finally, under the lantern's faint light he flipped open the grimoire to the passage on astral projection, analyzing it carefully. He looked up to see Micah fully asleep. It was amazing what that guy could sleep through.

After about an hour the same noises started up again from Lady Crow's room. Umbra tried to ignore it as he slid the grimoire under the couch and curled up again to try and sleep.

It seemed like forever as Umbra waited for the sun to rise.

When it finally emerged, light peered around the folds of the ragged curtains hanging on the dirty windows.

Finally, Micah rose out of his comatose sleep and rolled over, rubbing his eyes and yawning. "Had another nightmare did you?" he inquired.

Umbra nodded; his eyes darkened and puffy from the fatigue.

Sure enough Umbra was tossed out of the shack by Lady Crow without breakfast to go fetch firewood while Micah was to receive "special training", whatever that was.

It was tough to find firewood, it was a swamp after all, dry wood was scarce and something was always waiting in ambush. There seemed to be nothing but slimy trees and soft ground everywhere as Umbra trekked off down a hill.

symbol on his hand and concentrated as it lit up. "What the . . .?" Robyn queried.

Umbra sprinted towards her and grabbed her crossbow with his illuminated hand then adeptly slid through the muck to get behind her. The crossbow lit up a bright white and sizzled with immense heat.

"Ahh!" yelped Robyn, dropping it into the mud. Umbra quickly grabbed a nearby stick and whispered an incantation, the stick reformed into a spear in a flash of red light. "So that's how it's going to be?" Robyn frowned as she drew a cleaver from behind her back.

There was a multitude of weapons at her disposal, Umbra gulped. She charged at him swinging her cleaver wildly, Umbra was barely able to parry her blows as his wooden spear started to buckle under her relentless assault. The spear was breaking apart!

I need to finish this fast!

He rolled out of the way and with one hand reached for a handful of salt to perform a blinding spell on her. Before he could do so she rushed and sliced across his arm. His sleeve fell off and the scar on his hand was revealed.

"Argh!" grunted Umbra as he clutched his arm, blood trickled down. *She is good!*

He was running out of ideas. *Maybe the twenty-four hour death spell,* he thought, but he realized she would most likely chop him up anyway.

Robyn returned her cleaver to its sheath and drew a razor-sharp steel boomerang; it glowed with an eerie blue aura. It had been enchanted! Umbra's eyes widened.

"I hope you've made your peace!" Robyn declared as she tilted her arm back to toss the boomerang. Umbra turned and fled, his arm still dripping from its wound. His movements were getting clumsy as he stumbled on exposed tree roots and dips, the boomerang whistled towards him.

Suddenly Umbra had an idea. He dived into the nearest marsh, hiding in the slop and mud.

I hope this is worth it.

The boomerang flew straight past him, before turning to return to Robyn's hand. It clanked as it landed in her gauntlet. She stepped forward out of the green mist, scoping out the slimy trees and rotting wood around her.

"I'll find you, necromancer!" Robyn yelled, her growling voice echoed. The wildlife itself dared not stir. Umbra remained hidden in the muck. There he lay silently. After a few minutes Robyn went to look elsewhere. "I'll find you fiend!" she called out, as she walked away, disappearing into the green fog.

SIX

LATER, AFTER WAITING FOR a long time Umbra emerged, and cleaned himself off with a little magic. He sped off back towards Lady Crow's shack, hoping not to bump into Robyn on the way. His arm still throbbed from the wound even worse—he was getting light-headed as he dodged the twisted branches and exposed roots of the mire.

The house finally appeared through the fog as he raced over to the old wooden porch and peered in through the front door. Lady Crow hadn't bothered to close the door when she left.

"There wasn't much point worrying about theft in this swamp; nobody in their right mind would trek out here to steal all this dusty old crap," Umbra muttered, tying off a black scrap of cloth around his arm to cut off the bleeding.

"Hello?" Umbra echoed from the threshold, peering in with squinted eyes. No sound. Nobody was home.

I wonder what this special training is. He thought as he sped off towards the training ground.

The training ground was simply a small, relatively dry clearing within walking distance of the shack.

"Now boy, make a circle with that blood vial!" Lady Crow instructed Micah, her voice was a little deeper than normal. It was almost like she had a cold.

Umbra peered curiously from behind a nearby bush. Micah was obediently making the circle.

He held a long bone in his hand. *Was that a human femur?!* Umbra wondered as Micah laid it out in the middle of the strange spell circle he had carved into the ground.

"Good, Child! Now you just need a drop of your own blood on that bone and the ritual will commence," Lady Crow urged. "You will have that weapon you crave in no time."

Lady Crow was abnormally enthusiastic about this. Umbra thought as he spied her poised stance. She was normally apathetic to them, rarely showing any interest in their successes.

"And you're sure this will help me save Lydia?" Micah inquired nervously from the center of the array. Lady Crow nodded reassuringly.

"Don't stop now, you're so close!" Lady Crow insisted.

What is she so eager about?

Micah's blood hung on the edge of his palm for what seemed like forever, until it finally it dripped onto the circle. The very instant that tiny crimson droplet landed the array lit up brighter than the sun with an erupting flash, Umbra covered his eyes. He felt the massive surge of power knock the breath out of him with a fierce gale.

Once the light dulled and he looked again there was a massive, scaled grey demon standing cross-armed in the circle. Micah had hung onto the wet ground just barely clinging on inside the circle, the howling winds ceased to relent.

Umbra froze, recalling his own encounter with the contract demon, Belphagor. The world around him lulled as his own mortality came to mind; he struggled to catch his breath. His deal would come to term soon, and he didn't have much time left, less than a year in fact.

"What do you want?" boomed the demon over the loud howling of the residual winds, its eyes lit up as it looked down at Micah. Lady Crow stood contently at a safe distance with a peculiar smile across her face, she had been totally unaffected by the volatile reaction of the ritual. She stood unrelenting against the fierce winds, her purple shawl and grey hair fluttered furiously behind her.

"Make me a soul-bound weapon to grant me power to channel my magic and smite evil!" Micah declared at the pitch of a yell to be heard over the gale. As he held up the blood-stained bone; the demon sneered, raising its eyebrows with curiosity.

"Evil, you say?" the beast roared and flexed as the bone in Micah's hand glowed white hot. "Ouch!" Micah cried as his flesh seared and he dropped the bone. As it landed, a curious small stream of white energy seeped through Micah's mouth and swirled around the bone at his feet. When the bone cooled, it had changed completely. A Black-silvery obsidian blade lay at the young sorcerer's feet, still pulsing with pure energy. Runes were flashing an eerie blue, stretched across the length of the blade.

The horrific memories of the Night of Flames and his foolish deal with the contract demon returned to Umbra in a flash as he was reminded of Belphagor's sinister, dead eyes. That evil grin, those ruthless intentions, he can't watch his friend repeat his mistakes!

Umbra finally snapped back to reality, realizing what Micah had just done. "Nooooo!" he yelled as he dashed into the fray, the winds still whipping past him, almost in an attempt to slow his movements, but it was too late—the deal had been made. "That's his . . . soul in that sword!" Umbra stuttered, freezing on the spot.

The howling gale was gone as quickly as it had appeared; only the echoing evil laughter and dispersing smoke were left of the demon as it vanished.

Micah picked the sword up in awe. "It's so light," he scanned it curiously. The world around him seemed to be holding its breath nervously as he held it out.

Umbra could hear a muffled whisper echoing all around the training grounds, the kind of feeling that made the hair on your neck stand up.

"Now this soul weapon . . . Does that mean it has my soul or does that mean something else?" Micah inquired. Lady Crow nodded, casting a mischievous grin at Umbra.

"A small piece of your soul, to bond you with the blade," She clarified. "Be sure to keep it safe. Its power is yours alone, but whoever wields it wields your soul too." Lady Crow explained in that deep voice again. "Now people will try and take it, friends, enemies alike. You must be prepared to defend it with your life, my apprentice."

Umbra couldn't take it anymore and erupted. "Micah what have you done? You fool! Do you realize what you have made?" Umbra was furious. "That is your soul there, when you die what do you think will happen? Do you really want to exist as an inanimate object?" Umbra picked him up by his collar with his good arm. "Those demons always are deceptive in their deals! You know why I'm here; I thought you would know better!"

Micah's eyes widened. He glanced over Umbra's shoulder to look at Lady Crow. "You didn't tell me that! What do I do now?" Micah stammered at Lady Crow, who stood a few feet away with her arms crossed, glaring at Umbra.

SEVEN

A N UNEASY TENSION WAS looming that night. Umbra was once again plagued by restlessness, his injured arm bound tightly in cloth.

Micah, just as Lady Crow had planned, had become obsessed with keeping his sword safe, his paranoia had grown since the ritual. He insisted he sleep with it sheaved, his arms wrapped around it.

Umbra couldn't shake a feeling that sinister forces at work, Micah and he were caught up in the middle of something big.

That sword gave Umbra a cold feeling of dread he couldn't deny.

So there he lay in darkness in that dusty old house contemplating his next move, watching the iron chandelier sway in the breeze.

Micah was sound asleep and hugging his sword in its sheath like a pillow.

This weapon is making him crazy. Lady Crow must be lying! He hasn't been acting normal ever since he got it!

Whatever was going on here he was determined to figure it all out.

He reached under the couch to extract the Grimoire Demonus and carefully picked up his bag of ingredients. There was no sound tonight down the hall, it was silent as a tomb.

He skulked past Micah, who was mumbling something or other, it was unintelligible however since his face was buried in a couch cushion. Umbra grabbed his lantern and tiptoed down the hallway careful not to step on any squeaking floorboards.

He had memorized which ones they were; this was not the first time he crept around the house. It was usually to pilfer food though, this time his reasons were more important.

Pictures hung on the hallway walls; they seemed to contrast the gloomy theme of the house. They depicted a smiling woman and family all embracing. Their clothes were curiously old-fashioned.

Umbra finally reached Lady Crow's bedroom door. The snoring emitted from the room was far deeper and drawn-out than normal. Umbra's suspicion grew as he carefully turned the handle and opened the door. This ritual would provide him the answers he sought.

As he carefully opened the door and set up his ingredients, his hair stood up on the back of his neck. A cold feeling flowed through his bones; getting stronger the closer he stood to Lady Crow.

Opening the grimoire to the page he needed he reread it carefully. He quietly scattered salt in a ring around her bed and opened the blood vial he had in his pocket. With a small paintbrush he sketched the complex array on the floor, sure to follow the grimoire's instructions. He looked down in satisfaction at the complicated array he had sketched.

Finally he grabbed a copper goblet and sprinkled dried herbs, salt, and importantly the dragon's bane into it. The last thing he needed was a drop of human blood from the host.

This will be difficult, how do I get some of her blood without waking her?

With a small sewing needle, he cautiously pricked Lady Crow's fingertip. Her face scrunched up but she remained asleep. Once he had enough blood Umbra swirled it around to mix it. He scanned the grimoire and recited the passage, the contents of the goblet began to sizzle and boil. The vapors smelled strongly of blood, it turned his stomach. Luckily he only had to inhale the vapors and didn't need to drink the disgusting concoction.

He swirled the goblet around under his nose and took a deep breath. When he exhaled he was floating above his body, feeling as light as air. His body below was frozen in an exhaling expression. He felt light as a feather, now he had to climb into Lady Crow's head.

It was a bizarre feeling to need to 'swim' to someone and settle into their body, but he managed it. All of a sudden, he was hit with a flurry of images!

There was a young woman, Lady Crow. Only then she was known as Bella, she had a loving husband and two small children, a son and daughter. They lived in a small hamlet like the one Umbra had grown up in. Their modest little house stood on the top of a windswept hill surrounded by cornfields.

Bella had gone out on her own into town for groceries. She skipped care-free, a serene smile on her beautiful face as she strolled down the cobbled street. She warmly greeted the people as she went. Her modest sky-blue dress swayed gently in the wind imitating her thick, golden-blonde curls.

Modest little brick houses lined the street. Colorful stalls dotted the market place, though few were shopping today. She had picked up a few fruits, some potatoes, carrying them in a small hand-basket.

She reached one stall, but there was no food on display. Only a cloaked old man sat there, a crystal ball in front of him. It was something about him that drew her in. His eyes were grey as slate and seemed to stand out over his other features.

"Sit my dear, I shall read your fortune," he offered with a friendly smile on his face. Bella, curious of fortune-tellers and psychics sat down without hesitation.

The man reached out and clasped her hands, closing his eyes. The crystal ball hummed and began to shine. Everything around them seemed to freeze and dull, people were moving at a snail's pace now and everything was gloomy and grey.

All of a sudden in a sharp gesture the man's grip tightened and his eyes flicked open.

No pupils! Just like Lady Crow the night before!

Umbra continued following the images. "Yes, a fine model. You will please my master, Apathy," the man hissed with an evil grin. A strange insignia similar to a crescent moon lit up his forehead.

He leant back his head and opened his mouth, throwing his hands towards her and gripping her neck. Frozen in fear, she couldn't defend against him as moved his open mouth closer to hers. Thin, black strings of thread-like essence extended, flowing from his mouth and flew up Bella's nostrils after encircling her like spider's silk.

The man collapsed and the surrounding world returned to its vivid color. Bella stood straight up, dropping her groceries. Her eyelids flickered as she walked back towards her house.

The man lay face-down on the table, the crystal ball still humming. Bella continued walking back to her house.

Umbra looked on in confusion. *What just happened?*

Bella stepped into her house through the open door, her face sporting a blank expression; like she was asleep.

Lady Crow's frown grew deeper. Micah raised his sword, lifting Umbra's chin. "This is your last warning! Don't make me do this!" he pleaded.

"This is crazy, she's a demon! We HAVE to get rid of her!" Umbra persevered.

"Are you going to let him talk about me like that?" Lady Crow growled. Micah shook his head.

"You're lucky that we're friends or I'd slay you right now! Leave now, Umbra!" Micah ordered, delivering the ultimatum. The sword glowed with an eerie red light.

Umbra dropped the fire poker and hung his head, his pleas failed.

"You don't realize how much danger you are in!" he warned with concern in his eyes. Micah pointed the sword at the door, staring Umbra down.

The tension in the room was thick enough to cut with a knife and Micah's was definitely capable.

Umbra finally yielded, submissively slinging his bag over his shoulder. He stomped out of the ramshackle house, and made tracts to the nearest town.

He wondered if he would see Micah again as he squelched through the marshy wasteland towards Myst City.

"You did the right thing boy," Lady Crow assured Micah. They stared out the door at Umbra as he disappeared into the distance and out of their lives.

Micah let out a sigh of sadness, he would miss his friend.

Lady Crow went to stand on the porch, a grin crossing her face as her eyes flashed a solid white. Micah dropped his sword and sank back into a chair; the gravity of what had just occurred hit him like a wall.

Oh Umbra. Why did you have to do that?

NINE

U MBRA HAD FELT EVIL growing back in his former-teacher's
shack. He continued away from the home he had known for
two years.

He only had eleven months to break the demonic contract on
his soul and save himself from the pit

How will I learn enough to confront Belphagor now?

Umbra stood there for a moment contemplating the gravity of
his situation.

It had been hours since Umbra had stormed out of Lady Crow's
cabin. The foggy swampland and marshy ground were long behind
him now.

His black cloak flowed in the brisk wind; he scratched his scar,
covering it back up with his glove.

If anyone were to see that mark they would trace it back to
the incident in Brie. The case had become famous in the past few
years since he left, he had even heard about it from the odd passing
traveler he encountered in the swamp.

The tall pines rustled as they towered over the needle-choked ground below. The trees stretched like poles into what seemed like an infinite void, the ground view only broken by a few outcrops and ledges littered with a damp moss.

Umbra's visibility was quickly fading as the sun sunk over the wispy clouds in the west.

Before too long the moon had crowned and the winds picked up, stirring up the pine needles. Umbra decided to himself that he must be ready, this was dangerous territory. He no longer had the protection of a powerful sorcerer like Lady Crow and wouldn't be able to defend himself if the slayer returned.

He looked around desperately for a road; it would be his best chance to make it to the nearby city safely. He grabbed a nearby fallen branch, peeling it down to a bare stick.

A simple crafting spell should do it! He thought as he dripped a little of his blood vile onto the wood. He whispered an incantation and tossed the stick up in the air watching as it lit up an eerie purple light.

When he caught it again it was a long spear topped with an iron tip. He had chosen to fashion a skull on the blade just for a little flair.

This should fend off anything dangerous.

A little more confident now, Umbra strolled forth towards the small dirt road that emerged into view. He hoped to find shelter and plan his next move once he reached the city. Hopefully he could remain anonymous amongst the crowds of the city.

The wind rustled amongst the canopy, breathing life into the fallen needles as he closed his eyes in deep concentration. He was determined to kill that demon in Lady Crow, rescue Micah and he had to somehow get back his soul from Belphagor, the contract demon.

Two years had passed since he had fled Brie and he was still plagued by that same recurring nightmare. *That demon had tricked him! Any amateur necromancer can raise a zombie! He wanted his mother!* He was still so full of hate and humiliation for making that fool-hearty deal.

My time is running out!

What he was planning would solve everything, but he was unsure of how to go about it. His training was surely over. He wouldn't get any help from Lady Crow anymore and who knows what she was doing to Micah.

He looked over the horizon of trees upon the majesty of nearby Myst City. The tall, intricately-designed spires stood tall and majestic as the sun set behind them. The walls shone like polished marble and the city looked pristine. The artistic buildings graced the skyline and the sheer height of them was humbling.

Night was in full bloom now as he continued onward; the glassy eye of the moon spied him from overhead.

Umbra had heard rumors circulate that the forests surrounding Myst City were teeming with werewolves, it was the original reason the city was fortified.

I hope they are just rumors! Umbra continued onward, his fear setting in.

He finally reached the road, it was as dead as a tomb, the road was worn, but not a soul was present.

Clutching his robe as the brisk wind blew he started walking towards the direction of Myst City being sure to keep up a quick pace.

"Hoooooooooooooooooowwwwwwwwwwww!!!!!!!!!!!!!!!!!!!!!"

Another followed shortly after, it was closer though; another, then another.

The noises were all around him; he ran for a felled tree and ducked behind it trying to get a view of what he was dealing with. Umbra knew he couldn't outrun a werewolf. He planted his spear down nervously and reached for his blood vial to make a protection circle.

The needles rustled and within an instant a wolf shot right past his hand from behind, tearing the vial right out of his grip along with most of the glove concealing his scar. The wolf landed perfectly next to him in a hunched position.

Crowds of werewolves were snarling, vicious. Drool dripped from their blood-soaked mouths.

A few more appeared dragging a mutilated corpse with them, still being picked at by a few of them, they ripped and chewed furiously once the second the body had halted.

"Hooooooooooooooooooowwwwwwwwwwww!!!!!!!!!!!!!!!!!!!!!!" the creature boomed as it arched its ragged, fur-torn back. It spun around and eyed Umbra; its solid black eyes were so cold and dead.

It had already emptied the vial, the blood dripping down the beast's cheeks.

On the trees all around now werewolves clung. Their razor-sharp claws easily piercing the thick bark.

One after the other they lunged at Umbra, who barely managed to dodge each one. His fatigue was becoming apparent as his movements went from acrobatic, to nimble, to lucky, to clumsy.

He would not last long, and his spear was useless. They were too fast for him, he couldn't get a firm swing at them, and without his blood vial he couldn't use his magic.

I'm going to die here he realized. He was about to relinquish his defense to the merciless beasts. "Do your worst," he muttered.

Suddenly he had a revelation. He ran his hand down the spear tip, bleeding out his finger.

The pack around him snarled and grunted; their smell was unholy.

They smelled like rotten meat, dragged through a swamp.

Umbra tossed his cloak to the floor and planted his spear in the earth. He scribbled a small array on his arms and crossing them over his chest. He lit it up with a red aura.

This trick was used by Micah many times to boost his speed when sparring with him. He was lit up dimly now with a red glow, he extracted a small dagger from his pocket, clenching it in his hand. Assuming a defensive posture he readied himself to retaliate.

The largest of them, presumably the pack leader arched his back and readied to jump, his mouth was salivating like a hungry dog. Before it as able to lunge, an arrow whistled through the air and emerged through his forehead from behind.

The werewolf sizzled and burned as it collapsed in a limp heap, reforming into a ragged, naked man.

Silver Arrows!

Three figures riding horses stormed into the scene out of the fog, plowing down the beasts. They were led by a knight covered in shining armor riding a majestic black stallion. He wore an over-tunic bearing the emblem of Myst City and clutching a gleaming sword which he wielded with ease. Slicing and dicing the foolish werewolves who leapt at him, adeptly decapitating them one after the other, his horse snarled as it arched to kick away an attacking werewolf.

The werewolves returned to their human shape as they drew their last breath. The archer that had delivered that lethal blow to the pack leader rode behind him. He wore a tan-colored woodsman's hide suit and a plumed admiral's cap, firing arrow after arrow at blinding speed striking the werewolves between the eyes every time, dropping each to reveal a ragged, miserable person.

The following rider was a young woman wearing navy-blue robes and carrying a rune-covered staff. Her blonde hair flowed majestically in the wind and her blue eyes shone like gems, complementing her revealing azure robe.

Umbra's jaw dropped, almost forgetting the chaos and death all around him. The world lulled, the fighting seemed distant.

He had never seen such a beautiful woman, not since . . . He shook his head and dismissed the familiarity he saw in her.

She cast blue bolts of magic from her staff taking a few werewolves down. The magic acted like water and seemed to scald them on contact.

"Watch out!" yelled Umbra as a werewolf lunged at her knocking her off her horse and away from her staff.

"I'm coming, Marin!" yelled the knight as he spun his stallion around to move back to her, but he was blocked off by a pack of snickering werewolves and was preoccupied by their merciless assault.

Umbra, without hesitation ran towards her, sped up by the red aura spell he had cast.

She wrestled underneath the snarling beast, its drool dripping with anticipation; her face was scrunched up in fear.

Umbra's scar lit up with a red glow as he clenched his fist. The werewolf was tugged back, falling to the ground and struggling. It was being attacked by its own shadow!

The blackness enshrouded the werewolf until it stopped flailing, then dispersed, leaving only a charred skeleton behind.

The remaining dozen werewolves backed away in fear, fleeing in all directions. Umbra ran over to help Marin to her feet.

What just happened? I couldn't do THAT before! He thought as he dusted himself off.

She smiled shyly at him; he looked so familiar to her.

"Thank you sir, what is you're name?" she inquired gently as her eyes locked with his.

"It's Umbra, are you okay?" he replied.

Her face froze like she had seen a ghost.

"Marin, get away from that monster!" ordered the knight, Umbra turned around to see the archer was aiming his weapon right at him.

"Marin?" Umbra exclaimed his attention focused on her.

"Are you listening, boy?" the knight demanded as Umbra turned back to face the arrow pointed at him. Umbra was not about to chance dodging his shot, he had seen just have effortlessly the archer had taken down the werewolves.

"Gladius, Fletcher! Please! He saved my life! Surely you won't punish him," Marin pleaded as Umbra raised his hands in resignation. One hand was still bleeding as his aura faded, but the scar was still glowing wildly.

Marin stepped in front of him, arms outstretched. Fletcher lowered his bow with a drawn-out sigh. "He is . . . my friend," she explained.

Gladius removed his helmet and raised an eyebrow. He looked into her eyes, a solemn expression colored his aged face.

"We won't execute him, he doesn't deserve that death. But no heretic walks in this kingdom unchallenged!" he recognized the insignia on Umbra's hand immediately.

Gladius returned his sword to its sheath. His dark matted beard rustled in the strong wind. A scar lined his cheek, presumably from a past battle, his face showed signs of age. He glared at Umbra menacingly.

"The courts will decide his fate," Gladius dictated. "You will come with us, you abomination. I suggest you don't resist or we'll put you down like we did with the rest of these monsters." He motioned around him, the forest floor was littered with the corpses of former werewolves, he held up his gauntlet, stained red.

Fletcher dismounted and walked over to Umbra with suspicion in his eyes.

"None of that funny black magic, you!" warned Fletcher as he put Umbra in iron cuffs, Umbra could feel that they had been enchanted by someone very powerful.

Marin looked at Umbra and mouthed "I'm sorry" to him as she obediently followed the troupe. Umbra was cuffed and led back to Myst City what he could expect there was nothing but hostility.

His life lay in the hands of the courts now. The scar on his hand was still lit up like an ember and glowed eerily.

Great! I have a glowing piece of evidence on me now!

TEN

U MBRA WAS LED DOWN the marble floors of Myst City's court chambers; he was caught in awe of the majestic columns and stone statues towering over him. The hall looked ancient, yet well-maintained.

Golden torches lined the pathway lighting the room, if he wasn't being dragged to what was likely his death he would have stopped to examine the art tapestries all around him, knights with swords, archers with bows, axe-men.

Fletcher and Gladius led him down the walkway occasionally jabbing him when he slowed.

"What happened to you?" Marin inquired breaking the tense silence. "The day after your mother's death, I thought you had died during the night of flames! You dropped off the face of the earth, and then months later I arrive to see you being carried off by an angry mob and hanged! How are you even alive?" Marin demanded, reluctantly following Umbra and her comrades.

"Is this true?" inquired the judge, gazing down at Umbra. Umbra nodded with a fixed gaze of conviction.

The judge turned and huddled with the others around him whispering among them. He turned back to Umbra. "The penalty for practicing the arts of heresy on our lands is execution!" he decreed.

The Executioner-bailiff grinned at Umbra.

The judge continued: "But, in lieu of your actions to save a beloved member of our taskforce—The Golden Sun, you are to be imprisoned until we decide otherwise. Court adjourned" the judge banged his hammer.

"What the hell? I am not a criminal!" Umbra yelled, furious with the verdict.

"That's ridiculous!" Marin protested as the citizens murmured and the crowded room began to disperse.

"With all due respect, your honors, was I not spared for thievery in this very court and assigned to defend our lands alongside Gladius and Marin?" Fletcher inquired standing firm beside Marin, placing his hand on her shoulder. He was referring to his previous life as a pickpocket.

Umbra desperately looked at the Judge hoping him to revoke the sentence.

"Court will continue tomorrow morning after careful deliberation! This outsider is no son of Myst City as you, Fletcher," the judge decreed. His peers filed out of the chamber casting glances of suspicion at Umbra and Marin.

Gladius, who had remained seated and indifferent throughout the entire preceding stood up and left the chamber without uttering a word; his mail jingling, and his red cape flowing behind him.

Umbra was bound and led towards the jail block by the smirking bailiff.

"I will set you free Umbra, I just know it," promised Marin, a tear in her eyes. She mouthed "I'm sorry" as she left the room. Umbra pretended not to notice.

Umbra wasn't optimistic of his freedom as he was led down a bricked stairway and into a dreary jail block. The light dimmed around him as he descended the stairs.

The room smelled foul as he reached the end jail cell and was shoved into it roughly.

The straw floors and low, bricked ceiling were as confining as any cell could be. The one barred window overlooked the cobbled streets outside. The other cells were empty.

Umbra was left alone as the bailiff strolled off merrily.

I'll just use some magic! Umbra grinned once the room was clear.

He was about to conjure a spell to escape when he noticed marks etched into the iron bars. *Binding spells!*

The bars had been enchanted by a very powerful sorcerer he realized as he touched them, feeling the resonating energy.

He hung limply on the cell bars and let out an exasperated sigh, "Great! Just fantastic!" he groaned.

ELEVEN

"Thishttps plan is foolproof!" a cloaked old man cackled as he held the reins of a horse-drawn carriage loaded with straw.

The carriage shook as it rattled down the cobbled road toward the Myst City gates.

It had been a whole day since Umbra's trial and the sun was setting overhead with darkness ominous. The tall pines and looming threat of the werewolf-infested woods meant naught to this traveler; he was the dark force gathering.

"You had better be right!" threatened a tall, beautiful woman in a winding black dress.

She stood amongst a small crowd of similarly dressed people atop the large golden bails. The group was pale as snow and skinny as withered beggars.

Her stare was fixed forward, completely unaffected by the rickety road or gathering wind.

"Lydia! Are you sure we won't get caught by the guards? Sure we are hungry for blood and haven't eaten in several nights, but this isn't a good idea," warned a slim young man named Vlad. He had a looming presence about him. He was wrapped in a flowing black robe and his pale skin stood out in the emerging moonlight.

Lydia was easily the strongest of the whole group, and the entire clan was fiercely loyal to her.

"Lydia, now you have been our leader a long time now," Vlad began. "We are vampires, we know not fear. We hunger and thirst. But, even more importantly we are family, isn't that right everyone?" he exclaimed casting an affectionate glance at her.

The other vampires cheered when the gate emerged in sight, licking their lips with anticipation.

This small group of survivors was the remnants of the Dark Claw, the most notorious of vampire clans. Since the Golden Sun had begun guarding the lands further around Myst City, prey was harder find. Many of their brethren had died at the hands of the taskforce, even more of starvation.

"You had best hide, we're nearing the gates. If the guards see you before we are inside we are finished!" The old man warned in a hissing voice, reptilian in nature.

This man had unexpectedly appeared and struck a deal with Lydia, promising to escort her clan into the city for 'his own reasons'.

Vlad had convinced her to take up the offer since the clan was in such bad sorts and he was desperate to recoup their losses to rebuild the clan. They were planning a feeding frenzy and to turn the stronger citizens into vampires.

"My appreciation, Cassius, your talents serve us well." Lydia complemented as the vampires slid into the hay stacks to hide.

The guards were clad in steel armor and standing at attention by the gate house. They nodded politely and opened the gates without hesitation as the hay wagon came close. Cassius cast a mischievous glance as they passed.

Lydia had a bad feeling about tonight; she could almost sense disaster would strike in Myst City.

"Gladius, it isn't right to keep Umbra locked in that terrible cell. He saved me," Marin pleaded. Fletcher nodded in agreement.

She had protested since they left the courtroom. Finally, Gladius assembled them in the Golden Sun chambers to discuss the matter in private.

"She's right boss. Marin owes her life to that boy, heretic or not," Fletcher implored stepping out of the shadow.

The members of The Golden Sun were standing in the center of a circular marble chamber. The moonlight poured in through the open windows, the doors to the chamber were locked to conceal their discussion from the city guards.

A large Sun banner hung on a tapestry, illuminated by the open window. The tapestry displayed the great deeds of the Golden Sun's ancestors.

Their taskforce had always been small and dated back beyond memory. There were even legends that they fought against Zuul herself.

Gladius stared longingly out the window to the street. He spun around to look sternly at is comrades. "The King's court holds authority over us; the King himself will be at the next tribunal. The final decision will be his!" he ordered.

His mail jingled under his sword's sheath and crimson cape. He hadn't removed his armor since the battle and was still spattered with werewolf blood. His gauntlets were crimson from the blood spilled.

"We have bigger problems currently. There are rumors that the Dark Claw vampire clan has been sighted nearby. Our guards are few and since the battles with the demon lord Greed's armies we lack defense." He growled, referring to the failing northern campaign.

Gladius stared out the window down onto the snoozing twilight town below.

The demon lord Greed had been at constant war with them since he had conquered the former capital city to the north and settled there, he hadn't pressed forward for six years until recently.

The Capital had been raised in a single night by Greed's armies, the citizenry massacred, and the land destroyed. Since then Greed set his sights on Myst City.

"We could hire some of the citizens as militia," Fletcher suggested.

Gladius shook his head. "Nobody will fight against vampires, I'm afraid if these rumors are true we're in serious trouble," Gladius replied mournfully.

"I have an idea!" perked up Marin with a beaming smile.

TWELVE

"SQUEAK!" A RAT SCURRIED past Umbra's foot as he stood in the damp, straw-covered floor of the jail cell. He kicked a stone and it darted out of sight.

Umbra stomped around the cell impatiently as the moon rose outside. The moonlight illuminated the cell as he sat down on the simple wooden bed, his head in his hands.

He heard footsteps approaching and expected to see the fat jail guard with rotten teeth, who had been taunting him. The blue-robed figure that emerged was a pleasant surprise.

"Marin?" Umbra stood up, a look of surprise on his face as he walked over to the front of the cell.

With a shy smile Marin reached the cell. She was carrying the keys!

They jingled on her belt as she stood in front of Umbra. Only the bars separated them. Umbra's eyes caught hers as she turned the keys and swung the door open.

"But I thought . . ." Umbra began. Marin stopped him with a kiss.

Umbra was shocked by this, but he had wondered what it would be like for years. Closing his eyes he lost himself.

When the realization of why Marin had arrived set in she jerked back.

"What's wrong?" Umbra inquired.

"I came here to ask for your help," Marin began.

By now the streets were in chaos as citizens ran hysterically in all directions. Marin and Umbra emerged from the jail block to the outside street. The street lamps flickered as the people fled. The streams of blood outlined the cobble bricks and noises of terror and pain echoed all around.

Umbra had no idea what was going as Marin tugged his hand and ran towards the town square.

Women and children all around were screaming. Pale corpses lay against walls and in alleys as Umbra and Marin ran down the darkened streets.

At last they reached the town square, a huge stone building, where a mayor's citadel sat. In front was a well-trimmed lawn. Several town guards stood there, their matching steel armor and pikes glistened in the moonlight. Their faces covered under helmets made them seem inanimate as Umbra and Marin arrived. Gladius was walking past the lines issuing orders.

"Your enemy will be all around. They will attack without mercy. Do not spare them, remove their heads or stake them and above all: DO NOT show mercy," Gladius dictated as he drew his long-sword and donned his helmet.

Marin and Umbra walked up to Fletcher. He was crouched, checking his arrow-heads behind the formation. He looked up.

"What took you two so long?" he inquired. "Gladius seems to be fired up. He didn't notice you were absent yet, so don't say anything to him." Fletcher stood up, threw his quiver over his shoulder and adjusted his hat, the plume swayed in the wind.

"I hope you're ready Umbra, this will get messy" he warned as he walked towards the front of the lines to stand beside Gladius, ready to march.

"Marin, where are you?" Gladius called. Marin stuck up her hand and walked Umbra to the front of the line, their cloaks flapped behind them as the wind picked up.

The soldiers turned to gawk at Umbra as he walked past them. They whispered amongst each other.

"Did you bring the heretic?" Gladius inquired as Marin emerged from the crowd. Umbra stood cross-armed glaring at Gladius, his anger apparent.

"Gladius! Umbra is offering to help us. We owe him our respect at the very least!" Marin snapped as she grabbed a small vial from her pocket.

Gladius turned stubbornly and faced the troops.

She threw the vial against the ground. It smashed and water vapor rose. When it had dissipated Marin was holding her long wooden quarterstaff. It was lined with glowing runes and tipped with a blue gem.

One of the nearby guards reluctantly gave Umbra a steel pike then returned to formation.

"Move out, troops! Stay in at least groups of two! These vampires aren't to be underestimated!" Gladius ordered.

"Vampires?" Umbra's jaw dropped. Marin reassured him, clasping his hand.

"We can do this, you'll get a pardon, and you can go free" she assured him.

The troops dispersed in all directions, their armor clanking as they ran. Within moments the town square was empty. The sounds of conflict were heard in the nearby alleys and streets. Only Marin and Umbra remained.

"Where to?" queried Umbra, testing the weight of the pike.

"Follow me!" she called back as she ran towards the marketplace.

A bolt of hot water flew at a vampire's face scalding his eyes knocking him backwards. Marin's sapphire-tipped staff hummed as it recharged.

Umbra rushed the vampire with his pike and buried it in his shoulder. The vampire stood up, totally undaunted. Umbra pulled out the spear and jumped back to Marin.

"Any ideas?" Marin whispered standing at Umbra's side.

"My pike needs a little juice, but I lost my blood vial in the woods!" Umbra whispered in a hushed voice.

The vampire, now fully recovered lunged at him with a hissing noise, his face scrunched up to reveal his fangs, a glistening white. The vampire was salivating like a feral beast.

Marin dodged to the left and Umbra speared him in the chest, stopping him in mid-air.

Only small grains of dust fled the wound, this vampire had not fed in a long time.

The vampire grabbed the staff of the pike between his hands and snapped it off, landing perfectly on his feet. His black cape settled behind him. He pulled out the pike-head with ease, tossing it to the floor. His face blazed with anger as he glared at the two sorcerers with his silvery eyes.

Umbra and Marin looked at each other nervously as the pike-head rattled on the cobbled street. The vampire pounced at Umbra once again, hissing wildly, eager for blood.

"Noooo!" Marin wailed out as the vampire flew through the air.

The scar on Umbra's hand illuminated once more like it had done in the woods. The broken pike quickly reshaped into a steel scythe crackling with a black aura.

Umbra quickly dodged to the side and as the vampire passed he swung down and cleanly decapitated him like an executioner.

The swing took a lot out of him. He fell back onto his knees in relief. The limp figure continued flying straight into a wall with a crunch.

"That was amazing!" beamed Marin as she ran over to Umbra to help him up.

"How'd I do that?" Umbra stuttered, looking down at his wildly glowing scar.

"Well look here, a pair of two-bit sorcerers," Lydia echoed from atop the overlooking roof Umbra and Marin.

She leapt down landing effortlessly on her feet making no noise. Her pale skin glistened in the moonlight. Her cold, dead eyes glanced at Umbra's glowing brand.

She looked familiar to Umbra, but he couldn't quite place his finger on it.

Suddenly he realized who the devilish vampire was.

"You're Micah's sister!" he concluded, pointing his scythe. Lydia clapped with contempt.

Micah had rarely mentioned her, but from what he knew she was the right age, and looked very similar.

Micah was always been vague in detail of her, and now it was clear why he had kept silent.

"So you know that sentimental, foolish brother of mine! He's wasting his time!" she spat back at Umbra as she flourished herself to him.

She was wrapped in a revealing black gown. Her pale face and silvery eyes glowed in the moonlight. Her fangs were much larger than the other vampires.

"I know who you are, Umbra and I know you are friends with my brother," she grinned.

How does she know that?

Umbra and Marin assumed defensive stances. Lydia began to pulse with dark energy as she flexed her lean muscles.

I can't kill Micah's sister

"We don't have to do this!" Umbra insisted as Lydia prepared her attack.

She was ready for blood, nothing would stop her.

FOURTEEN

MEANWHILE, MICAH WAS STILL honing his skills in Heartless Swamp. For days now he had pushed himself further with his training.

He was growing more and more impatient.

He wondered every day whether or not Umbra was right, or if it even mattered. Lady Crow was teaching him the skills needed to confront his sister, Lydia.

Does it even matter if she's evil?

He remembered his sister fondly. They had been separated since Lydia was taken by vampires, that was several years ago.

Since then he arrived to train with Lady Crow a few months after Umbra had. Lady Crow was always a harsh teacher but since Umbra left she was a lot more accommodating, even gracious.

Recently he asked about a vampire cleansing ritual so he could find and heal his sister.

His sister was a few years younger than him and their parents had passed away. He had been left to care for her but he had failed.

He carried the weight of that failure heavily, and blamed himself for the people who died because of it.

One day when hiking in the woods they were ambushed by a group of vampires. One had knocked him out and when he awoke Lydia was gone.

He had searched for her for months; following rumors of a female vampire of her description creating havoc in various towns. By the time he'd arrived to those places she was off terrorizing elsewhere.

She had become the leader of the Dark Claw vampire clan and quickly earned a reputation as a brutal monster.

Micah knew this but was determined to save her and return her to the innocent sister he still loved. He realized he'd need to subdue her and know the appropriate rituals to heal her.

That is why he sought out Lady Crow.

He was desperate, but as long as she could teach him how to heal his sister and give him the strength to face her, did it matter if she was a demon?

A sinking feeling had been growing ever since Umbra had left. Lady Crow was pushing him more each day. The lessons had become grueling and excruciating.

He was sure he was near the end of his training and would be ready to confront his sister, Lydia.

Today he was attacking dummies and dodging tombstones in a cemetery while moving at high speeds.

"Faster, boy! You won't defeat anyone with slow slices!" Lady Crow called out as Micah swung his soul sword at the dummies he had fashioned with magic. "Let's try something else!"

Lady Crow raised her hands and began pulsing with dark energy releasing a black mist that absorbed itself into the ground.

The ground trembled around Micah and skeletons rose from their graves.

They groaned and cracked as they struggled to unearth themselves. Before long they were out and standing ready.

Lady Crow raised her hands once more and with a loud bang and more black mist weapons appeared in the skeletons' hands.

She pointed at Micah to issue the attack. One after another they stormed him, swinging their maces, swords, axes, and other weapons at him, grunting and moaning as they moved. They weren't fast but they were very skilled with weapons. Micah suspected these were once soldiers.

"Ah!" Micah yelped as an axe cut him across the cheek.

"Get angry! That's the only way you'll win! Harness the dark magic within you!" Lady Crow instructed, standing firm out of the fray.

Micah's temper was rising as the skeletons chuckled at him. He swung wildly at them but was parried by their weapons. They regrouped to begin attacking him in pairs.

He dodged them effortlessly. His cloak was browned by soil and his collar red from his bleeding cheek. He tried to focus and become angrier.

He pictured his sister being taken away and the vampires that had overpowered him so easily. As his focus grew his sword began to glow red, the eerie blue runes marked across the blade were replaced with different, crimson markings.

The blade pulsed in his hands, a red aura surrounding him. He charged the skeletons swinging his sword, the red light illuminating his face.

His blade cut through one skeleton after another like a hot knife through butter. Even as they blocked with their weapons his sword plowed through them.

"Marin! She doesn't need to breathe! You have to try something else!" Umbra exclaimed. He was starting to panic, Marin was powerless against her.

The water dropped off Lydia's body and Marin began to channel another spell through her staff. She hummed with a blue aura as she gathered her strength.

Lydia turned sharply at Marin and motioned her hand violently; Marin was flung at the wall, knocking her head. Marin's staff was pulled right out of her hands and flew to Lydia, landing perfectly in her palm. Lydia pointed the staff at Marin to blast her with her own spell.

Umbra couldn't let her do this. He bolted over towards Lydia running on adrenaline. With one swift motion he swung his scythe down breaking the staff before it could launch the spell.

The staff split in half, the gem sizzling out. Lydia, dropping it swung a fist at Umbra connecting with the back of his shoulder with a wet cracking noise.

Umbra howled as the searing pain shot through his body.

The solid hit to the shoulder had dislocated it. One arm hung limply next to him as he clutched the scythe with the other.

Grimacing from the pain he swung at Lydia with his scythe, which proved unwieldy with his one good hand. Lydia swatted it away effortlessly and landed a punch right in Umbra's stomach, he gasped for air as he collapsed to the ground.

Lydia snapped Umbra's pike in half with almost no exertion and dropped the fractured pieces to the floor in front of Umbra. They rattled as they settled on the cobble street.

Umbra looked on in horror as Lydia strolled casually up to Marin with her claws tensed, and her fangs visible. Marin groaned, rolling over but unable to get up.

"Good-bye sorceress, it's been fun," Lydia began as she lifted her foot to step on Marin's neck with her heels.

Nooooooooooooooo!

All of a sudden Lydia's expression froze; a red cut appeared through her neck as her head slipped slowly off and fell to the floor followed closely by her body.

Umbra was on his knee where he had fallen, his scar glowing wildly and a red aura pulsing around him. He swung his hand again in a chopping motion and Lydia was sliced cleanly down the middle as a web of black streaks segmented her.

Umbra let out a sigh of relief coupled with a groan, the heavens began to pour down on them. His powers were growing, but he didn't understand why.

The soothing rain washed the blood from Lydia's body and sparkled on Marin as her aura returned. Her powers of revival in rain healed her. She climbed slowly to her feet.

Running over to Umbra, she helped him up, cradling him over her shoulder.

He moved his wet hair aside to look down on Lydia's body and let out a sigh of relief, but also a feeling of immense guilt.

Micah, I'm sorry, I had no choice . . .

The screams from the city had dissipated and cheers rang out from the soldiers. The conflict was over.

"Thank you! Thank you!" cried out an old man, running over to shake Umbra's good hand. His other arm still hung limply at his side.

Umbra smiled weakly and nodded. Marin looked contently into his eyes as his dark hair clung to his face. The rain was lashing now, but they were just glad to have survived.

The old man ran off joyously to inform the other citizens. However, once out of sight, the man stepped cautiously into a back alley and with a grunt of pain pealed back his skin. A pale, reptilian-like man stepped out of the folds and stretched his arms in relief. The old man, Cassius, now in his real younger body stepped out of the alley.

He was a young man, with a green tint to his skin. He tensed his body and cracked his knuckles.

"Ahhh, it feels so good to be out of that shell," he beamed. An evil grin formed across his face. "Time to sow some mischief in Heartless Swamp!" he smirked, walking off into the dark, shaded back alley. The rain gushed off the roofs as he strolled through the downpour, his mind on his next task.

SIXTEEN

GLADIUS AND FLETCHER ARRIVED on the scene, their faces drenched by the downpour. "What happened here?" Gladius inquired. He scanned the scene, eyeing the two vampire corpses.

Fletcher had raced over to the fallen soldier to check his pulse.

He shook his head and sighed deeply.

Marin was still cradling Umbra over her shoulder. "Umbra killed these vampires and saved me! One of them was the clan leader!" Marin explained with intensity in her eyes, although half hidden behind her soaked hair.

Umbra stepped away from Marin. "One second," he promised as he snapped his shoulder back into place.

His face tensed in pain, then relaxed to relief as he moved his arm freely around. "Pretty good for a heretic wouldn't you say, Gladius?" he smirked, hiding the dull pain.

"Good work. I suppose you have earned my respect for now. I 'll sort out your case with the courts. You are free to come and go as you please," Gladius replied with a nod of respect, concealing his uneasiness.

Fletcher likewise patted Umbra on the back. "Good work kid!" he complimented.

Marin's smile beamed. She hugged Umbra enthusiastically.

"Let's go sort this out with the tribunal," Gladius spoke stiffly as he turned to walk back to the judge's chamber. Fletcher tipped his hat to Umbra. He smiled at Marin, turning and followed Gladius.

"Umbra, I noticed you having trouble controlling your magic. We should go see my mentor, the wizard, Astralode. He'll surely help you," Marin promised as she led Umbra towards the old district of Myst city.

The old district was thick with smoke. Blacksmiths were hammering iron on anvils around hearths, sweat pouring off them; the raindrops sizzled off of their hot brands. They stopped their labor, greeting Marin as she strolled past them.

The cobble streets were worn and cracking as they neared their destination—an old brick tower. When Marin reached the stone doors, she waved her hand. Runes lit up around the doorframe and the door swung ajar.

The circular room inside was crammed with bookshelves wall to wall with a large winding staircase in the center of the span.

Tables and candles levitated in the air, their intricate designs were whimsical, gold swirled patterns and gem-encrusted.

"Astralode! I have someone here to see you!" Marin called up the stairs.

Sure enough an old, bearded man descended the stairs. He wore a purple velvet cloak and a crooked wizard hat. His white beard and jovial, aged face contrasted the solemn expression branded on Gladius'.

"Marin, my dear!" he smiled as she ran to embrace him. "Who did you bring for me today?" he inquired curiously.

He walked towards Umbra and shook his hand, noticing the burnt scar almost immediately. "Judging from the black cloak I'd say you were a necromancer."

Umbra nodded. Astralode closed his eyes and concentrated, still holding Umbra's hand. "Hmm, there is a lot of untapped power coursing through your veins, Umbra. I have one serious question I must ask you . . ." Astralode paused with a solemn expression on his aged face. "Are you Marin's boyfriend?" he inquired with a goofy grin.

"Astralode this is serious!" Marin exclaimed, her face as red as a tomato. Umbra was taken aback by Astralode's bluntness, and shook his head slowly.

Astralode released Umbra's hand and strolled casually over to his book shelf to extract a book. "Give me one second, I need a refresher. How did that astral projection spell go again?" he asked to himself, putting on his reading glasses and opening the book.

"Salt, blood, and Dragon's bane!" Umbra chimed looking curiously at Astralode.

"Brilliant! My lad, this old man tends to forget things sometimes," he replied with a cheesy grin. "Okay, well you have the blood. I have some salt somewhere around here, and dragon's bane . . . well I don't have any of that."

A look of disappointment crossed Umbra's face. He had left the dragon's bane with Lady Crow when he <u>left</u>.

"Don't worry!" Marin beamed. "Astralode is brilliant, he can just conjure some!" she exclaimed with a smile.

"Oh that reminds me, I was scrying with my crystal ball when you were attacked by those nasty vampires and I saw that you broke your staff," Astralode piped up. Marin nodded.

"Well I can always make you a new conjuring vial, my dear," he smiled as put his hand on her shoulder and walked to the stairs. "You should come too, my boy. I keep all my ingredients upstairs in my study."

"Isn't he great?" asked Marin cheerfully.

How did I get stuck with that old hag, Lady Crow as my teacher? Umbra pouted as he followed them up the stairs.

SEVENTEEN

BACK AT HER HIDEOUT Robyn recalled the events of her clash with Umbra.

Her cleverly concealed refuge sat nestled in the rocky peaks of the Rumble Mountains. From this secret keep she had a clear view of the area below. A carefully placed bronze telescope allowed her to track targets with ease, even at distance.

She had thrown her chainmail armor on the stone floor of the bricked fortress, which resembled more a prison block than a home.

The stone floor was cold to her bare feet when she kicked her boots off, but she didn't mind.

This retreat was her sanctuary, her refuge.

The weapon racks against the wall were crowded with glinting steel and silver. Her arsenal was massive. Over the years she had collected every possible weapon she could need during hunts.

Trophies lined the walls, frozen in macabre horror. Werewolf heads, vampire teeth, zombie hands, and drake horns were nailed to wooden plates.

One trophy in particular was the focal point of the room. It was her most treasured possession—the spearhead of the weapon that had killed Zuul.

She believed the legends and kept the relic on display to remind her why she became a slayer.

She had tested the point in battle, but curiously it could wound and stun a demon, but not kill it.

She remained certain that only when combined with its staff would it gain its infamous power.

She was a proud slayer, destroyer of evil and all threats across the land. She saw it as her personal mission to cleanse the land and bring peace. Trained in every form of combat, and every weapon, she fought with brutal efficiency.

Her desire for perfection was her greatest strength but was also her greatest weakness. She took failure seriously and Umbra's escape stung her like a deep cut.

She admired her athletic physique in a full-length mirror, wiped her blood-dotted face with a wet towel.

After Umbra gave her the slip in Heartless Swamp she made her way back here. Her contract to kill Umbra had been a failure. Not to be defeated so easily though, she would bring his head to her client. A strange old man she met in Myst City who had paid her with a strange, jeweled amulet.

After a long, contemplative bath in her makeshift washtub she stepped out wrapped in a towel, feeling reenergized. Donning her clothes and armor, she stared thoughtfully at her weapon cache and rolled the odd amulet in her hand.

There were rumors that Umbra was in Myst City. He was now totally exposed with no protection from his mentor.

What a golden opportunity! She gleamed as she selected her weapons.

She chose a few swords, a dagger at her ankle and a small crossbow.

She took a deep breath and stepped out of the door with a clear goal in mind, the setting sun lighting up her armor as she walked casually down the mountain path.

The gathering wind whipped past her fiery red hair, her equally searing gaze was fixed on the roadways below.

"Welcome to my study!" Astralode announced jovially pushing open the mahogany doors to reveal a mind-bogglingly large library.

Umbra's jaw dropped. The book shelves were three-stories tall at least! There was enough books in this chamber to fill a lake, every one sorted and lined up flawlessly.

White, satin-gloves levitated past, sorting the books; many moving stepladders floated around. The skylight above illuminated the majesty of the pristine library.

The marble floors sparkled as more floating white gloves mopped and polished them tirelessly. In the center of this surreal room stood a round oak table covered with open scrolls, books, and papers Astralode had been reading.

The gloves had ignored this table as they continued cleaning tirelessly. One glove however lay still in the middle of the paper pile. As Umbra approached he heard quiet noise of snoozing. "Is that glove sleeping?" he inquired, perplexed by the thought.

"Oh, that's just lefty!" Marin explained looking endearingly at the odd familiar nestled on the table. "I tried to make a helper hand like Astralode's. He didn't really come out right," she giggled.

"Hmm, let's see here," Astralode rummaged through the papers before extracting a dark leather-bound book with a lock on it. He chuckled lightly as he slid a paper carefully out from under the snoozing glove being sure not to awaken it.

Umbra's eyes drifted across the table to a familiar tome lying open. "The Grimoire Demonus!" Umbra announced as he spotted the book. "How did you get one of those?" he demanded.

Astralode peered over the small lenses of his reading glasses, his smile sobering. "You think in this massive collection of books I wouldn't have a black magic section?"

His smile returned with a chuckle. He pointed up at the far corner shelf. Occult icons lined the shelf and gothic candlesticks levitated nearby setting the theme of the section perfectly.

Marin approached Astralode and peered at the occult tome in his hands.

"So this will do what for Umbra?" she inquired with a confused look.

She looked to the small recipe shelf by the wall and walked over to it hoping to find the ingredients they'd need. "So we have salt, we got some snake's blood . . ."

"It needs to be Umbra's blood!" Astralode cut in. Marin cringed as she gazed at him.

"I don't see any of that dragon's bane stuff around here; it's that red and pointy plant right?" Marin continued as she rummaged through the various jars of weird and wonderful items.

Some morbid, others bizarre, the shelf was crammed with countless reagents. The shelf smelled strongly of formaldehyde, Marin didn't seem to notice as she excitedly browsed through the inventory, almost knocking over a jar of pickled lizard eyes.

"Nope, Astralode. There isn't any dragon's bane here," Marin concluded. She turned to face Umbra solemnly.

"We can always conjure some!" she beamed, her expression quickly brightened.

Astralode signaled to one of the white gloves. The magical glove stopped working instantly and floated over to him.

"Please would you find me my conjuring recipe book?" Astralode asked.

The glove obediently flew over to the shelves, making sign language gestures to the other gloves nearby. They directed it to the central top shelf.

Umbra was astounded by the incredible arcane display.

"You really have to show me how to make those," he affirmed in amazement.

Astralode grinned, stroking his beard as he watched the glove find his book.

"It gets hard keeping track of where I put most of my books," Astralode admitted. "The helper hands remember where they are and perhaps clean up a little too obsessively. They are my finest creations," Astralode boasted watching the helper hand reach the location of the book. After extracting it, it descended slowly and handed it courteously over.

"Thank you. Take a break for a little while if you wish," Astralode suggested. The helper hand gave a 'thumbs down' gesture and continued working. "They never want to stop," Astralode sighed as he glanced at Marin's familiar, Lefty, snoozing on the table.

Umbra and Astralode skimmed through the book together looking for the ingredients to conjure dragon's bane. Marin sat at the edge of the table humming to herself, her boredom apparent.

One of the helper hands offered her a glass of water. She moved her blonde hair aside to reveal a wound on her neck. Dipping a finger in the water she let a few drops fall onto the cut, it healed instantly.

Umbra had been watching, pretending to read with Astralode, he was astounded.

"It's called water healing, one of Marin's best talents. She's near unstoppable with enough water around," Astralode explained fully aware where Umbra's attention lay.

"I tutored her myself since she arrived here as a small child. She was naturally adept in aquatic magic, so I focused her training to hydromancy," he explained.

Astralode looked affectionately at Marin. "I myself am somewhat of a jack-of-all-trades. But in a hydromancy fight I'm sure this great sorceress could win," he chuckled, she pouted lightly.

"How much do you know about necromancy?" Umbra inquired.

Astralode's smile faded. He looked at Umbra with a stern face.

"Enough to not dabble in it my boy," he responded "and neither should you." He sighed, "Sure, your shadow magic may be impressive but you must set healthy limits. The best necromancers have become corrupt monsters from abusing that power."

Umbra had heard all this before; he nodded and rolled his eyes as Astralode continued lecturing.

"Right here!" Umbra pointed excitedly at the page. "It says one part toad bile, one part swamp worm, three parts blood spores." Umbra looked up to see Marin already rummaging through the recipe shelf.

"Got it all!" she announced as she placed the various jars and beakers on the table.

Astralode continued with the passage, once he had finished he put the book down. He tightened his grip on his walking cane; standing up straight he closed his eyes with intense focus.

A silvery aura surrounded him and his cane began pulsing with magic. The room lit up and the cane reformed into an elegant magician's staff, silver with gold trim.

When the light in the room faded Astralode was standing firmly on his feet, wielding the staff. His eyes were silvery grey and his robes now as white as snow. He had an aura about him. His skin had a hint of glowing vitality despite his age.

He held his hand over the table, the ingredients lit up in a silvery array that appeared on the floor.

In his hand appeared the steaming goblet. "Now a drop of your blood if you please, Umbra" he requested holding out the goblet.

EIGHTEEN

MARIN STOOD OUTSIDE OF the array nervously watching the ritual unfold. She had never seen a full-blown shadow ritual before. Although curious, she was still unnerved by it.

Umbra squeezed one of the wounds he had from fighting Lydia until a small droplet fell out into the goblet. Astralode swirled it around, his face serious and intense. He motioned for Umbra sit in the center of the array.

"Now just relax . . ." Astralode's voice echoed. Umbra drifted off to sleep as the spell took affect. The last thing he saw was Astralode taking a whiff from the goblet and then darkness.

Marin watched as Umbra slept and Astralode stood as still as a statue. She wondered what was happening inside Umbra's mind and whether her teacher would succeed.

There she sat and waited for about an hour, she was about to fall asleep when she heard a shout.

"No! This can't be!" *It was her teacher's voice!* His body and lips weren't moving. The noise seemed to be coming from Umbra.

Marin ran over, shaking each as she tried to wake them, it was fruitless.

She looked around frantically until she saw a large pot of water and bolting over to grab it she almost stumbling over.

Once it was next to the array around Umbra and Astralode she whispered an incantation and swirled her finger in the water. The water rippled to reveal a clear image of Umbra. He was younger but she knew it was him.

Marin watched carefully as the memories continued, trying to figure out what was going wrong. There were flashes of a fire, death and destruction.

The Night of Flames!

The visions continued with a lonely young man deep in study of a dark revival ritual. So too she saw the encounter with the demon. The images then began moving too quickly comprehend clearly.

The water began to boil, the pot heated up scalding Marin's fingers. "Ouch!" she yelped jerking them away. She squinted trying to see through the steam of what was unfolding below.

Out in the shadows of the forest the vampire Vlad waited.

He had managed to escape Myst City in all of the confusion and chaos of the midnight feeding frenzy. He had eaten a helpless elderly couple and a small child.

He had lost his love, Lydia that night, waking from his slumber this night was like reliving the loss. They had gotten separated in the frenzy.

He had always admired how powerful she was, how she was as fierce as she was beautiful to him.

He remembered back to when he first met her.

It was a dark night in Fuchsia village almost six years ago.

He had recently been initiated by the Dark Claw back then. They were deliberating as to which house they would target for their feast that night. They all hovered over the town below from rooftops like reapers choosing their next victims.

Normally a town would be on high alert if they heard that the Dark Claw were nearby, they were the strongest of the vampire clans. But they had managed to sneak in undetected

In those days the clan was thirty strong, but as the years passed and more of them fell in combat and starvation their numbers dwindled.

It was back then when he first met Lydia.

She was an orphaned girl with an older brother. Vlad was young himself at that time, vampires age to around thirty then stop. As long as they were fed they could live forever, but their hunger for blood was relentless.

He was so infatuated with her and insisted that the clan spare her from their "random picks".

Unfortunately, later that night Lydia and her brother were walking in the woods, gathering firewood when the clan decided to ambush them.

The vampires were perched high in the trees watching the two victims below. Vlad had protested repeatedly to their leader to spare Lydia.

"We either kill her or initiate her!" the leader told him.

Vlad decided on the latter; they could be together forever if he did.

So when the order came he was sure the clan didn't kill her or her brother. The clan attacked them and over-powered the two siblings. Her brother was taken down first as Lydia could only watch in horror.

The clan wanted blood but Vlad wanted them alive. Just before the fighting became lethal he questioned their leader, Veracious.

"I want the girl to become one of us, her brother too," he pleaded.

The leader had sensed the girl's great potential and allowed Vlad to take her off to be initiated. Much to the discontent of the other vampires, Veracious ordered them to look elsewhere for prey.

Lydia's brother was left for dead by the other members. Vlad knew he was alive, he had felt the boy's great potential.

In a clearing not too far away Vlad huddled over Lydia.

"Are you okay?" he inquired as he helped Lydia sit up. "You had an accident and I rescued you; they would have killed you if I hadn't intervened," he explained. The vampire leader Veracious had altered her memories of the attack with the little magic he knew.

"Who are you? You look familiar," she whispered, still dazed. The moon was full and Vlad's pale skin was haunting, but Lydia was not afraid.

"Your brother ran off and left you to die in these woods when the vampires attacked," he had told her.

She was infuriated and upset by this. He had offered to initiate her by having her drink a drop of his blood. "You never have to be alone again," he promised her.

Over the years she quickly became the strongest vampire, Lydia later became the leader of the Dark Claw when Varacious was killed by a red-headed slayer.

Vlad was never able to confess his feelings for her, pretending to not have any. He admired her from afar as she grew into the most powerful leader the clan had known.

Everything was fine until that fateful night in Myst City when his world was turned upside down.

That despicable Necromancer! His blood, if he had any, boiled when hearing the name "Umbra". He hated him so ferociously. The only goal he had in mind now was to kill him.

The failure of the Dark Claw, the abandonment of the changeling Cassius and his own hunger didn't matter to him now. He only wanted revenge.

NINETEEN

ACK AT ASTRALODE'S TOWER, Marin was furiously trying to awaken Astralode and Umbra.

She had splashed water on them, slapped them, and shaken them. Nothing worked!

Yells and calls for help from her teacher still echoed from Umbra's head. Marin, in her desperation grabbed the goblet out of the frozen hands of her teacher and took a whiff of the concoction.

The effect was instant! Marin felt like the weight of her body had fallen away as she entered into Umbra's mind to find her teacher.

Astralode was frozen in front of a demonic image when Marin found him. The words "He's mine, leave now!" kept echoing around.

Marin was floating above an open grave. A blood-red demon was standing in front of the younger Umbra demanding his soul. She was horrified when he agreed to it and was branded on his arm by the demon.

Lady Crow's eyes were solid white and a sinister smirk formed on her old, withered face.

Cassius scuttled off to conceal himself in the undergrowth. Hiding like a beast in the muck and mud, entangled in the shrubs and bushes he sat and waited.

Cassius then wormed his way through the undergrowth of the swamp, gradually making his way towards Micah's location.

Micah had been sent towards the heart of the swamp to collect firewood, Lady Crow knew that a swamp ogre lived there but she wasn't worried.

Cassius scuttled through the tangled brush and slimy wood, his vision revealing only heat signatures, making his navigation effortless. He saw exactly where Micah was and he was closing in on him.

"Time to make some magic!" cackled Cassius as he hid behind a tree.

He bent over and tensed as his skin bubbled and crackled. It began to stretch and shape over him as sweat poured down his face and he scrunched his face in agony, the local wildlife darted away as panic hit them.

Finally he had finished transforming and was now a perfect clone of Umbra down to the last detail of fraying around the edge of his cloak. He emerged reborn as Umbra in almost every respect.

He could not however perform magic; he was a changeling not a sorcerer.

Beads of sweat ran down his cheek, he was exhausted from the transformation and he panted heavily.

Crouching down in the muck of the swamp interior Micah caught a nauseating whiff of something strange. He hadn't smelled such a stench before, it was almost sickening and it was getting closer.

He looked around at the mighty fallen trees dotted with fungi, the vines that entangled like constrictors, and the strange shapes moving around.

The mist was getting thicker and the stench stronger, Micah dropped his bundle of wood and drew his sword. The sword crackled with ferocity as Micah's tension grew, Lady Crow mentioned something might be out here but she wasn't specific as to what.

The stench became overpowering, the muck and mire bubbled like boiling stew. Micah with his sword at the ready, was prepared for whatever would emerge.

All of a sudden, the mire was silent, only the chirping of crickets was heard. The stench still remained strong.

"Come out whatever you are!" he demanded, looking around anxiously. The swamp seemed to be tensing for something drastic to occur.

All of a sudden a grime-covered log sailed towards Micah through the fog, which he split effortlessly with his sword.

A watery-gurgling growl echoed as a brown, grimy beast ran towards him. The hulking figure was wielding a greened wooden club, and was covered in muck and filth.

Its small yellow eyes were narrowed as it took its first swing at Micah. He dodging it easily, and the club smashed a tree nearby which fell down instantly.

Micah looked up at the monster. *A Mire-ogre!* He dashed at the beast dodging its clumsy swings and slid between its legs, severing his right ankle.

The beast buckled and howled deafeningly as it bled. The blood smelled even fouler!

Micah took off his glove to reveal a tattoo on his hand, a demonic symbol which he activated with a flash of black light. His muscles bulked and throbbed as his shirt ripped leaving only his flowing cape, his skin darkened to a shadowy blue as his eyes became a solid red.

The ogre covered its ears and moaned painfully as its ankle bled out.

Micah sprinted towards the crippled creature and swung wildly, his sword lighting up with an eerie red. Once he had passed by a few times crisscrossed lines appeared on the ogre as he fell apart into an unidentifiable pile of mangled limbs and flesh.

Micah was breathing heavily now and fell to his knees coughing and gagging. His body shrunk and skin returned to normal, his torn clothes hung loosely.

His feet retracted into his now torn boots and his body was beaded with sweat as his eyes returned to normal.

Cassius watched curiously from the tangled wood of a nearby felled tree. *A partial demonic transformation* he observed. Lady Crow must have really been empowering this kid.

"Perfect! He'll tear Umbra apart," Cassius snickered as he stood up to mimic Umbra and validate his clone-form of him.

"Is that the best you can do Micah?" called out Cassius in Umbra's form, his voice identical. He stepped forward from the mist. Micah was still on his hands and knees panting.

"Umbra?" he panted as he got to his feet, now covered in mud. "What are you doing back here?" he inquired.

"You are just as weak as your sister. I diced that vampire to little pieces. She was crying out for mercy but no monster deserves any!" Cassius taunted with an evil grin.

"What did you say?" demanded Micah holding out his blade. His fatigue now replaced with immense anger.

"Little Lydia is no more, nothing but a pile of scraps for the dogs to chew on. The perfect end for that monster do you think?" Cassius continued, Micah's anger raged.

"You killed her?! You're the monster Umbra! Lady Crow was right about you!" he blasted as he prepared to strike.

Uh-oh! He's mad now, but how do I get out of here alive? Cassius thought, being careful to conceal his fear.

"Now die!" yelled Micah as he stormed Cassius.

Cassius cart-wheeled to the right but Micah turned to attempt again. This time he managed to clip Cassius' side as he attempted to dodge.

"Ahh!" yelped Cassius as blood spewed out of his deep wound. He fell to his hands and clutched his side.

There's only one way out of this! He thought. He gargled spit in his mouth and waited for Micah to attack again.

Micah was fuming mad, his sword burned bright red and his expression matched it in ferocity. Cassius spat out a huge brown glob of venom that hit Micah in his eyes.

"What the . . .?" Micah yelped as he fell to his knees trying to scratch the venom out, he was blinded and vulnerable, at least for now.

"Didn't I tell you that you are weak?" Cassius taunted, finding his strength.

He walked up to Micah and drop-kicked him in the stomach knocking him flat, kicking his sword away then putting his foot on Micah's face. He pressed down as Micah struggled on.

"Huh?" Cassius looked down to see Micah's hand clenched around his ankle. "Ahh!" Cassius yelled as Micah squeezed and squeezed. Cassius struggled desperately as the blind Micah tightened his grip. Cassius' ankle cracked and buckled until skin was broken, the bone snapped under the pressure. Micah refused to stop as he continued constricting Cassius' ankle.

In desperation Cassius grabbed a nearby rock and smashed Micah's hand with it repeatedly until he let go, howling in immense pain.

Cassius now mortally wounded and in severe pain scurried clumsily off into the mist leaving Micah fuming with anger.

"I'll find you Umbra! Mark my words!" Micah yelled out as Cassius disappeared into the thick green mist.

Cassius was bleeding out fast! He needed to get back to Lady Crow to be healed; he had succeeded in his mission so she would have every reason to oblige.

TWENTY

"So my boy, I have unlocked some of your dormant power. You may notice that you no longer need blood for your magic, nor will your power manifest sporadically. All I ask is that you are careful with your new-found strength," Astralode counseled as he sat opposite Umbra and Marin around his paper-scattered study table.

The helper hands had already begun cleaning up the array and mess from the astral projection ritual.

"That demon, all that fire . . . What was that Umbra?" Marin stared intensely at Umbra waiting for him to answer. His head was buried in his hands.

"Well I . . ." he began, lifting his head to look at Marin. "I sold my soul that night and I need to find some way to get it back!" he explained. He scratched his scar before pulling a glove over it.

"Why would you do such a thing?" Marin demanded standing to her feet. "That's the dumbest thing you can do!" she turned and walked over to the ingredients shelf.

Astralode just sat with his hands locked thumbing his beard in quiet contemplation. The argument raged on.

"Why do you care what I do with my life?" Umbra shot back at Marin as he walked over to her. His cloak clung to him.

"Is it so hard to believe that I care about you?" Marin replied without turning around. She was rummaging through the shelf looking for a staff summoning vial.

Umbra's eyes widened. "You care about me?"

"Of course, why wouldn't I? You big stupid jerk!" Marin pouted with a childish frown on her face.

"I intend to fix things, however I can. I just don't know how I'm going to kill that demon," Umbra reassured her and she embraced him burying her head into his shoulder.

"Then you will need the Spear of Destiny!" Astralode announced as the room fell silent. "The Spear of Destiny was a weapon used by the famous hero that killed demons eons ago. Rumor has it that it was in Greed's possession like much of the other ancient relics and treasures."

Gladius and Fletcher walked down the hallway from the senate chambers with a desperate uneasiness.

"Well, we know of the invasion plans for Myst City by the Demon Greed but what can we really do to stop it?" Fletcher complained as he struggled to keep up with Gladius' quickened pace.

Gladius' cape flowed behind him as he marched away from the senate chambers. The scout reports that had informed them of Greed's plans were trustworthy, he was just a little taken back by the grim news.

"Well, we must take the fight to him! We can't let *Myst City* become a battlefield!" Gladius decreed, freezing in his steps.

"How do you propose we go about attacking Greed's encampment?" Fletcher inquired skeptically. To face a demon was considered a death-wish. Gladius' scheme was dangerously reckless.

In the candle-lit hallway the plan was laid out.

"Well, let's start with what we know about him first," Gladius began.

"That Greed is a seven-foot tall killing machine?" Fletcher cut in. Gladius silenced with him a raised hand.

"We know he lives in an encampment in the northern ruins of the former capital, and we know he keeps company with all matter of vile beasts," Gladius continued.

"And all that treasure he supposedly hoards," Fletcher added.

"What valuables he may or may not have don't concern me Fletcher, we need to figure out a way to kill him!"

They were standing firmly despite their concealed anxiety.

"Maybe Umbra knows how to handle a demon. He is a necromancer is he not?" Fletcher suggested. Gladius raised his eyebrow and rubbed his chin before walking away thoughtfully.

"Where is he right now?"

"He is with Astralode and Marin," Fletcher replied.

TWENTY ONE

CASSIUS AGONIZINGLY DRAGGED HIMSELF through the mire. He longer was able to dodge the sharpened roots and slimy undergrowth as proficiently as before. He snagged his wound on the piercing claws and teeth of the bloodthirsty swampland vegetation.

He was bleeding out pretty quickly now and was scared he wouldn't be able to make it back to Lady Crow in time.

He fell through a sharpened snare of thorns landing painfully on the wet ground. He was starting to black out. *I have to get back to master!*

He dragged onward through the muck and slime like a shameless beast gasping for air. He finally reached a gulley. Lady Crow's house was on the other side!

A relieved, dizzied smile formed across the Changeling's face as he let himself fall down the muddied slope and roll to a stop a few hundred yards from his destination.

Lady Crow stood perfectly still on her old, wooden porch staring intently out into the wilderness of the swamp. She barely noticed Cassius drag his bleeding carcass up to the porch.

He had lost his Umbra skin but the wound had gone far deeper than that. His normal reptilian form was bleeding out just as bad. "Massster!" he pleaded reaching out to Lady Crow, who looked down on him with contempt.

"Did you finish your task?" she inquired coldly, ignoring his mortal wounds and immense pain.

"Yessss, master please help," Cassius begged, his head still spinning as he reached for her ankle.

Lady Crow smiled evilly, and looked down on Cassius. "Good, now there's one last thing I need from you servant . . ." she began as she held her hand outstretched to Cassius. Cassius looked up expectantly until he realized what she was about to do.

"Not my soul! Master Apathy! Anything but that!" he squealed as the white stream of his soul was drawn out through his mouth and collected into a small orb in Lady Crow's hand. Lady Crow admired the swirling white soul ball she held in her hand for a moment before she crushed it and inhaled it.

She felt a rush of exhilaration and cast a glance at Cassius' now dry, shriveled remains. She placed her hand on his skull and watched it as it melted into the wet ground along with the rest of his remains.

Unscathed by the brutal murder of her loyal subject, Lady Crow casually pulled up her old wooden chair and sat down contently awaiting Micah's return.

"Where is that fiend?!" demanded Micah moments later as he burst through the thicket appearing in view of Lady Crow, his sword clenched tightly in his hand.

Lady Crow stood up and called him over and innocently inquired as to what had occurred.

"Umbra returned! And he killed my sister!" Micah panted. "I confronted him but he blinded me like a coward and fled!" he raged as Lady Crow sat him down in her chair.

"Dear boy, I will help you," Lady Crow cooed.

"You will?"

"Of course, I know how you wanted to redeem your sister and restore her to normal, but that Umbra had to go and kill her didn't he?" she feigned grief.

She turned around and walked over to the small wooden table nestled on the veranda.

"It is fortunate he didn't kill you, we must make you ready to face him."

"Whatever, it takes!" Micah responded, his fatigue fading, a look of immense anger forming across his face.

Off in the northern wastes, nestled in the rocky ruins of the former capital city lay Greed's encampment.

He sat on the throne in the palace ruins surrounded by all the treasure he had stockpiled over the years.

Greed was a demon of insatiable voracity, sitting lazily on the tarnished gold throne as his skeletal minions stood firmly at his side.

He was a large, hulking beast with clawed hands and feet, and impressive outstretching wings. He clad himself in all the jewels he could find, worshipping himself like a god.

The ragged, skeleton minions wore the simplest of armor and wielded the most basic weaponry.

Three years ago Greed's army had laid siege to the town. The Capital was relatively peaceful and lacked the army to stand up to Greed's legions.

In a single night Greed's army stormed the town and committed mass genocide on all of its inhabitants, burning and looting as they went. The atrocities committed that night had become famous nation-wide.

Greed had a particular interest in the king's treasury; sure enough he was able to add its riches to his own impressive collection.

His lesser demon entourage marched up and down impatiently.

"Master, we must press onward with our campaign! This region holds nothing more for us. Myst City is ripe for the taking! Our scouts have discovered that it was recently ravaged by vampires and its defenses are cracked!" his main advisor Affluence insisted. He wore armor from Greed's treasury that sparkled in the specks of light that emerged through the gloomy, cursed sky.

No territory claimed by a demon flourished after occupied, the land itself seemed to die, the skies dimmed, and the air staled.

Greed sleepily spoke up. "The plan was to lure the Golden Sun here; the necromancer will surely follow them. He will come looking for this!" Greed reached into his treasure pile and extracted an amber-colored pole.

"What would he want with that? Although it is the Spear of Destiny, we don't have the spearhead. He can't kill a demon with that," Affluence questioned.

Greed glared at him, making him recoil. "I mean sir; surely he will look for the spearhead first."

"It is not our place to question, Wrath, he has commanded us!" Greed boomed as he stood up. The skeleton minions stood at attention and Affluence nodded his head in agreement.

For some time now Greed had wanted to take Myst City, he had heard not only was the town poorly defended but it boasted a sizeable treasury. He was waiting on orders from Wrath before he could make a move though.

The doors opened and a satyr strolled in with a bag over his shoulder. His goat legs beaded with sweat from running and his crimson body was dotted with perspiration. He shook his horned head and held a scroll out in front of him.

"I have a message from Wrath, your Excellency," the satyr messenger announced.

Greed waved his hand for the messenger to continue and stared at him while he opened the scroll and cleared his throat. "To demon lord Greed: I am pleased to inform you that Apathy has set the wheel in motion and driven the vampire's brother into confrontation with Umbra. Their fight will ensue very soon: as decreed by demon overlord, Wrath." The Messenger let out a sigh of relief as he rolled up the scroll to hand it to Greed.

Greed snatched it before reclaiming his seat at the stolen throne. The satyr saluted before leaving quietly.

The entrance door opened to reveal legions of skeleton soldiers and troll commanders standing at the ready.

"We are ready for his arrival," Affluence sneered as he walked over to a large map table in the middle of the stone chamber.

"Apathy had better be sure that the vampire's brother does not intervene before Umbra plays his role like Wrath has foretold," Greed snarled breathing his noxious sulfur breath.

TWENTY TWO

THE GIANT STONE DOORS of Astralode's tower burst open with a loud bang. The levitating candles lit up to welcome the new guests.

"Marin! Umbra!" Gladius called out, his voice echoing around the room.

"They must be upstairs boss," Fletcher suggested.

Gladius complied and the two of them scaled the spiral polished wooden staircase at top speed, their steps heavy from fatigue. Astralode, Umbra and Marin emerged into view as they reached the top and entered into the library floor.

Their reflections were seen in the polished marble floor beneath their feet. The floor shook lightly as Gladius' metal stirrups paced over it.

Gladius strolled over to the wooden table where the sorcerers were seated. They faced towards him, curious of what he wanted.

"I have a question, boy. Now you say you are a necromancer, correct?" he began, he removed his helmet and wiped the sweat off his forehead, his beard damp.

We're back on this again? Umbra rolled his eyes

Umbra looked up coyly, "As long as it's legal," he chimed, nodding at Fletcher in acknowledgement.

Marin stood to her feet following Umbra as he walked over to Gladius with a glare on his face. Astralode put his hand on Marin's shoulder.

"Leave them be," Astralode whispered in Marin's ear freezing her in her tracks.

Fletcher stepped between Umbra and Gladius, facing Umbra. "All we want to know is how to kill a demon, Umbra. We aren't here to start trouble. Isn't that right, boss?" trying to dispel the tension between Umbra and Gladius.

Astralode shot up to his feet. "Demonology? That is forbidden magic! Why do you come here and inquire about it?" he demanded glaring at Gladius.

"Don't they execute people for stuff like that?" Umbra feigned ignorance.

"Sit down old man!" Gladius ordered. "Umbra, do you know anything or not?" he demanded. Umbra eyeballed him.

Astralode frowned, whispering under his breath.

"Well, I too am trying to kill a demon. The only way I know is with the spear of destiny," Umbra retorted, walking slowly away. "Sealing them is one thing, killing them is something else entirely."

Fletcher and Gladius looked at each other. What choice did they have but to put their trust in this sharp-tongued boy?

"So where is this spear?" Fletcher questioned.

Gladius put on his helmet. "Greed has it I'm sure; he has pretty much everything else."

Astralode nodded in agreement.

"We can't face Greed with our dwindled number of soldiers, he has an army," Marin reminded them.

"Do you have any allies who will support you?" Umbra inquired; eager to get the spear. Astralode scratched his beard.

"Years back Myst City belonged to an ancient alliance—the Grand Alliance with Sunrise City and Plateau City. We battled as one against the hellish Demon, Zuul herself in the Twilight Wars," Astralode interjected.

"Perhaps that ancient alliance still has its merit between the kingdoms," he postulated, closing his eyes.

"There hasn't been friendly contact with them since," Fletcher sighed

"Then we must send messengers to prove our allegiance to the Grand Alliance and stand against Greed!" Gladius suggested, followed by approving nods from the room.

"But we'll have to split up to reach both cities in time," Marin fiddled with her hair. "Umbra and I will go to Sunrise City on the other side of Rumble Mountains in the east while the rest go to Plateau City in the west," Marin dictated.

"Then it is agreed, we'll split up to meet our allies and ask for their help. Once we have their combined armies we can finally destroy that demon Greed," Gladius decreed.

"I'm game, boss," Fletcher agreed, stretching his bow-string and adjusting his hat.

"Umbra and I are in," Marin declared.

Umbra didn't match their enthusiasm. "I . . . uh, we don't have time for this!"

"So what do you suggest?" Fletcher asked. Gladius frowned.

"If Greed has the spear I'll sneak in their and get it myself!" Umbra grunted, turning to walk away.

"Stop right there!" Gladius ordered his voice heavy with authority.

"Umbra, what you're suggesting is crazy," Marin exclaimed.

Umbra stopped cold. "Fine," he sighed. *Once I get that spear I'm breaking out of this contract!*

Astralode peered at Umbra, reading his thoughts. "Then it's in your best interests to help us then."

"Take this insignia, boy," Gladius held out his hand. A shining gold sun-shaped badge glistened in his palm.

"With this you can prove your connection to us." Gladius explained.

This is a mistake. Gladius thought to himself.

Umbra stared blankly at the insignia. Gladius saluted him before turning to venture west with Fletcher.

"Now we match!" Marin beamed, revealing her insignia. Umbra and Marin left the tower waving to Astralode as they went.

"I will be watching you on your travels and offer as much advice as I can. Be careful!" Astralode called as the door shut behind.

"About Gladius, he's not a bad man, Umbra," Marin assured him.

Twenty Three

T HE NIGHT WAS SETTLING in as Micah trekked the path towards Myst City, the only thing on his mind was revenge. Revenge for Lydia, his beloved sister who had been murdered by Umbra.

Every time he thought about it and Umbra's mocking smile back at the swamp when they had fought he clenched his fist. Kicking up his feet as he stomped angrily by, not hearing the rustling trees behind him.

The pale-faced Vlad clung to the canopy watching intently as Micah stomped past. He could smell the healthy blood pumping through Micah's veins. It smelled fresh and full of power; it was a soothing thought in his otherwise troubled mind.

Vlad dropped silently from the tree. His cloak flicked behind him like a black flag. He tiptoed up to Micah hoping to snap his neck and drink some much-needed blood.

"Freeze!" yelled Micah. He spun around with his sword outstretched.

Vlad froze in surprise and held up his hands submissively.

His speed! It was inhuman! Vlad thought to himself.

Micah glared at him.

"You're a vampire," Micah concluded after scanning Vlad. "Tell me what you know about Lydia!" he demanded. His sword burned a bright red terrifying Vlad.

Vlad sensed the raw power emanating from him. As great as it was, he knew Umbra's was stronger.

"I know she was killed a few nights ago," Vlad alluded.

Micah glared at him. *He knows something*

Micah lifted Vlad's chin with the sword tip. "You know where he is, don't you?"

"Who are you talking about?" Vlad inquired, playing dumb. He knew Micah was asking about Umbra.

Vlad had caught Umbra's scent from the night Lydia was killed.

Micah called his bluff. He saw the fear in the vampire's eyes. "You will take me to him," he ordered, his eyes piercing Vlad.

Wait, this might not be such a bad thing Vlad realized.

"You can't face him alone!" Vlad blurted out. "I have felt his power growing immensely over this last day. You won't stand a chance against him!"

"Why should I believe you?" Micah raised his sword again; the red energy had slightly faded.

"Because . . . I want to see him dead as much as you!"

Micah lowered his sword, his gaze still fixed. *Can I trust him?* Micah wondered.

"Why are you telling me this?" he inquired.

"I know how to make you strong enough to face him," Vlad promised.

Micah rubbed his neck nervously. "I won't be turned, so don't bother."

"I know a better way. You will be invincible."

Micah's curiosity peaked. He put his weapon away.

Vlad stared at the sword recognizing the demonic text; *she will know how to help him, surely.*

Gladius and Fletcher had mounted their horses and sped off east through the woods just as the moon was overhead. Their horses' hooves thumped on the stony road as they sped onward.

Micah saw them far off quickly approaching.

"We must hide!" Vlad alerted as he tugged Micah and leapt into the canopy of the nearest tree

The two horses galloped by unaware of the necromancer and vampire concealed above.

"I don't think they saw us," Micah let out a sigh. The two of them dropped adeptly to the forest floor.

Vlad's stomach rumbled. "I need blood!" he whined.

Micah grunted, tossing his blood vial to Vlad who gulped it down in an instant.

"Thanks, what may I call you?" Vlad inquired curiously.

"I am Micah," he grunted.

Vlad's eyes widened as he finally recognized him. *Lydia's brother!*

Without making a sound Micah continued on the trail with Vlad leading the way.

Micah's need for revenge burned like a pyre within him. *Umbra's pyre,* he thought to himself with a smile.

He would kill Umbra for what he had done, he was trained in very dark arts after Umbra left and he intended to use them.

The wind rustled in the trees animating the leaves and pine-needles, the dusk night held a great deal of tension over this precarious alliance.

TWENTY FOUR

THE SUN WAS SETTING as Marin and Umbra separated from Gladius and Fletcher. An uneasy feeling of dread crept through Umbra's bones.

Once he and Marin reached the foot of Rumble Mountains they took a moment to compose themselves before scaling this dangerous path. Sections of crumbling passes, razor-sharp canyons to fall into, dizzying heights, and dangerous conditions made this mountain range treacherous.

Their destination lay on the other side and they had little choice but to brave this hellish summit.

The road was well-worn from the traders using this route on foot. A skeleton lodged in a nearby rock pile was a keen indicator of how safe such a journey was.

Rumor abound was that a dangerous enemy resided in these peaks. Umbra knew they'd be fine since his new powers had been awakened by Astralode. He was as confident as ever, perhaps even over-confident. It was a strange feeling, but his blood pumped with magical energy, yet he still felt cold and empty.

The crystal tip of Marin's staff lit up forming a make-shift lantern as the sky darkened.

Umbra had his empowered pike at the ready. If they could slip by quickly they could make it through the mountains unchallenged.

Umbra felt the Golden Sun insignia in his pocket and sighed.

How did I get roped into this?

Only a few days ago he was on trial for his life because of them. Now he was obliged to help them.

Marin glanced back at Umbra who was beginning to trail behind.

"Do you need to rest Umbra?" she inquired careful not to make too much noise. Umbra shook his head.

"I was just thinking to myself," he admitted, raising his head and sporting a fake smile.

"I know this is overwhelming to you Umbra, but I have been on missions like this before," Marin reassured him.

"Horseback in these mountains is a bad idea so we are better off walking. It is safer. If you can call anything about this quest safe," Marin whispered as she fell back to Umbra's pace and held his hand tightly. Umbra smiled genuinely this time.

"Besides, who would want to mess with us?" he added with a smirk which was matched by Marin's.

They continued scaling the pass up the rocky peaks. Nothing seemed to grow on this mountain. It consisted entirely of rock, with the occasional boulder.

How could anyone live here? Marin thought to herself as she maintained her smile and pressed onward.

Now as dark as it was empty, Marin brightened her light. She was nervous it could be seen far off, but what choice did they have?

Umbra looked down over the edge of the cliff. Stone spears lined the shadowy canyon below, a terrifying sight to behold considering the erosion to the pass they walked. Umbra gulped.

After walking for a few hours Umbra and Marin finally took a rest by a nearby boulder. Marin planted her staff in a rocky crevice. Umbra rummaged through his backpack finally extracting a loaf of bread, tossing half to Marin.

Their eyes met, and blushing, Umbra averted his gaze.

"We probably shouldn't stop for too long, you brought your water vials didn't you Marin?" Umbra inquired between bites, feigning aloofness.

"Yeah, my regeneration spell will keep us energized so we won't need to sleep. I don't have too many vials so I should fill them when we reach some water," Marin explained.

Umbra rolled a new blood vial around in his pocket; Astralode had handed him for complicated arrays in emergencies.

"And we can contact Astralode whenever we need him with this!" Marin held out a clear, round orb.

"We are definitely prepared for anything," Umbra smiled with a relieved sigh.

Almost immediately an arrow flew through the air skimming Marin's arm, followed by a lantern thrown into the scene. The lantern smashed spilling a puddle of ignited oil. The entire mountainside was washed in light.

"Ahhhh!" she yelped, clutching it in pain. Umbra jumped to his feet.

"Who's there!?" he demanded, his pike at the ready. A small rock rattled above, before he could turn an unknown figure flew by and knocked him flat, winded.

It was the slayer!

"Fine by me, if you want to die I will be the one to deliver judgment," Robyn threatened raising her cleavers.

"Let's do this!" Umbra declared.

Gladius and Fletcher continued forth on horseback heading west towards Plateau City. Their horses' hooves rattled on the old road.

They were just about out of the territory of Myst City and reaching the border to Darkwoods, the pine trees were replaced by thick oaks. The night sky was blocked out the canopy. The moonlight only filtered in through small gaps.

Their fatigued horses slowed to a walking pace. The woods around them echoed with unfamiliar noises and the rustling of distant brush.

"Do you think Marin and Umbra are okay?" Fletcher called to Gladius, who was riding a black steed along side Fletcher's tan horse.

Gladius took off his helmet and nestled it in his lap. "I'm sure they are fine," he replied with his eyes fixed forward.

"They have a scrying orb from Astralode, he should help guide them," he explained.

Gladius knew well of Marin's prowess, she had been allowed into the Golden Sun taskforce as a young girl on recommendation by Astralode. She had proven herself time and time again in battle, killing trolls, werewolves, an ogre; her magic was very impressive.

Gladius considered her the daughter he never had, and now she was a young woman he was proud to call her a comrade.

He wasn't particularly pleased that she had gone along with Umbra but he respected her decision, even if he thought Umbra was untrustworthy.

"I just have a very bad feeling," Fletcher shivered. They reached a diverging road marked with an old wooden sign, dismounting to read it.

Darkwoods Outpost was to the left and Road to The Dying Lands was marked to the right.

"This is a no-brainer, Greed lives in The Dying Lands so we go the other way," Fletcher chimed. "Only problem is, the residents of Darkwoods Outpost aren't allies of Myst City at all! They were deserters during the Twilight Wars. They have killed many of our diplomats!"

"We seem to have no alternative. Hopefully they won't resist our passing if we are discreet," Gladius hypothesized, stroking his beard.

The soldiers of Darkwoods Outpost were supposed to come to aid The Capital when Greed attacked. Gladius had witnessed the town crumble and was one of the lucky few to escape; their allies had left them to die.

Gladius, resentful of their cowardice, was uneasy traveling though their shadowy territory.

"Let's go!"

He and Fletcher lashed their horses' reins. The horses sped onward into the sinister woods.

TWENTY SIX

T HE RUINS OF THE Capital hummed with activity. The ghoulish legions of the demon lord Greed patrolled endlessly through the ruined landscape of The Dead Lands. Evil was stirring as the demonic plotters debated their next move.

Greed was slumped in his golden throne, another treasure he had accumulated over the centuries. He cleared his throat and a silence fell upon the stone chamber. "The vampire's performing exactly how Apathy predicted," Greed chuckled as he stared into the scrying orb nestled in his hand.

"Once he reaches Lust's temple she'll strike a deal in our favor and we will be able to control him," Affluence added.

The demon lord Greed turned to face his advisors, rolling a coin between his claws. Their twisted bodies and unsightly appearance were as withered as the land surrounding Greed's haunt.

His leading advisor, Affluence crossed his arms and grinned evilly. "Not long now my lord, Umbra will fulfill his role."

"What about Gladius and the archer heading west?" inquired another advisor nervously.

"They are of no concern to me," Greed dismissed. "The rebels in Darkwoods Outpost will probably chop them up anyway," he predicted.

His advisors' faces beamed with glee.

The ruined castle glowed eerily, illuminated by torches depicting occult symbols. The pale blue lights cast these sinister markings. The moonlight from the exposed skylight glistened off Greed's prized treasure hoard.

Greed turned to his chief advisor, Affluence. "Begin moving a battalion east, we must keep Umbra on track. If possible we must halt his progress so Micah catches up to him," cackling, he pointed out the door, the skeleton sentry guards marched out the door mechanically as Affluence followed them.

The long tables of the immense mess hall were covered with brew and red meat. Lesser demons and trolls were stuffing their faces and drinking ale profusely.

"Groll!" yelled Affluence from atop the descending stairs. The mess hall fell silent and the masses stood at attention.

"Yes Sir!" replied a hulking troll, wiping his food-covered mouth. His grey skin was littered with small cuts and scratches. He had a huge gash over one eye and was clad in a leather harness and chain-mail tunic

"Gather your troops and take a squadron of bone soldiers and make your way towards The Lava Fields. You'll be given further orders to meet with an agent when you are within reach," Affluence dictated.

Groll nodded at the trolls and goblins sitting around him. A select few filed out after him as he marched out the doors into the courtyard where bone soldiers stood perpetually in formation.

That fool will surely fail, and that's exactly what we need Affluence thought as he watched the drunken stragglers stumble out the courtyard door to catch up to the division.

Umbra's scar glowed white hot as he clenched his pike. Black energy crackled around him as he tightened his grip on his weapon. He pivoted his foot in the rock and charged forward to clash with Robyn.

Marin stood nervously on the sidelines.

Why is he being so stubborn? She wondered. She fidgeted uneasily, prepared to step in if the fight looked bad for Umbra.

Robyn dashed forward, her blades sliced through the air savoring their target as they went. Her first blade whistled through the air missing its target, the other rattled roughly on Umbra's pike. Robyn's hand throbbed from the impact.

With an adept sweep, Umbra tripped her and stabbed down. Robyn rolled over, dodging Umbra's attack and swung her sword at him which Umbra jumped over.

The two of them dodged each other's blows with astounding agility, it was like watching an elegant dance as they flirtatiously attacked and dodged. Intensity grew in their eyes as they finally finished dodging and struck at each other, parrying the blows, locked in a struggle.

The soft dirt below was their arena and they were the fighters. They were locked in a clash to push one another back.

Umbra jiggled and scraped one foot on the ground. Marin's jaw dropped as she watched the array Umbra scratched in the dirt illuminate. Umbra leapt back as purple light shot up creating a dome around Robyn.

"What is this?!" she bellowed, banging on the now solidified magical surface of the dome.

"A containment circle," Umbra replied smugly. "It should fade in about twelve hours or so . . ." he stuck out his tongue mockingly. "Or was it twenty four hours?" he chuckled.

That should keep that psycho off our backs!

Robyn was banging furiously on the magic dome but the impact sound was buffeted, causing only ripples across the purple translucent surface.

"Umbra, that was amazing!" Marin beamed as she ran over to hug him. She held her still wet hand over his bruises and closed her eyes. They healed magically, amazing Umbra. They tiredly walked away to continue their trek.

"You can't just leave me here!" Robyn yelled from inside the circle. She was banging furiously.

"You can stay there and cool off for a while, catch up on some reading or something," Umbra suggested, ridiculing her.

"We must make haste, this is unfriendly territory," Gladius insisted as he and Fletcher both tightened the reins on their horses.

The horses upped the pace and approached a sprint, the sound of their hooves echoed around the dark forest. The noises of the forest fell silent, ushering in a growing tension.

"Look out!" Fletcher leapt off his horse, knocking Gladius to the ground as an arrow whistled by and implanted into a tree. The

"I have a bad feeling about this," Fletcher gulped as he looked at the fiery chaos.

What a mess! Gladius thought to himself continuing into the burning town.

TWENTY SEVEN

"**L**ISTEN UP SCUM! WE move out on my command. High Advisor Affluence has issued that we march to The Lava Fields immediately," Groll, War chief of the Troll division delegated as he marched up and down the lines of troops.

Goblins, trolls and skeleton minions made up the army. The goblins whispered amongst themselves, their grey-green skin was protected by dull iron helmets and armor. They carried rusted hatchets and their slimy drool dripped out of their concealing helmets.

The trolls were hunched over and hulking, their mail armor rattled as they groaned and scratched themselves. They wielded hammers and maces and were deftly trained to smash enemies with little exertion.

The armored skeleton soldiers stood lifelessly in perfect formation, their dull weapons held in identical fashion.

The overcast gloom of Greed's castle courtyard would instill an eerie sense of dread to even the toughest of soldiers.

Ravens sat atop broken stone pillars spectators to the devious schemes hatching below. The landscape of the courtyard was nothing but brown dirt; the glorious history of this royal castle which now lay in ruins had all but faded.

Greed himself had murdered the king of this once thriving capital and taken the throne. Within the space of a few years the land decayed, the buildings crumbled, even the dead rose to serve Greed. Greed's very presence there was a plague upon the land.

After the troll and War chief, Groll had briefed his troops he issued his second order: "Once we arrive we wait for the signal to meet up with one of our agents."

Evil grins of bloodthirsty anticipation dawned on the faces of the troops. The skeleton soldiers' eyes lit up an eerie red as they awoke to follow their General.

Groll, now wearing his black cape and dark iron armor donned his horned helmet and mounted his horse.

His horse was a conjured hell-steed granted to him by Affluence for the mission. The dark, semi-solid mare snarled and growled with sulfurous breath. Its blood-red eyes glowed eerily to strike terror into those who were unfortunate enough to face it.

Groll adjusted his horned helmet "Move out troops! To The Lava Fields!" the troops cheered at this command and marched out.

The ground beneath them shook from their heavy steps. From the tower above Greed watched with a satisfied smile as he watched the army sweep across the dusty plains around his capital.

As Gladius and Fletcher marched with the dark elves through Darkwoods the woodland around them watched ominously, almost anticipating the carnage to come. Giant spiders crawled into their burrows, the hell-wolves watched intently at the passersby and the ravens above cackled contemptuously. The entire woods seemed to be sizing up Gladius and Fletcher.

Finally the group reached the shattered barricades of the village. Old stone buildings packed together in this small stronghold showed signs of damage, cracks and chips on their walls and shingled roves. The streets were in disrepair and a stone fountain of a mermaid was chipped and cracked, the water trickled out of its wounds.

The group continued marching down this miserable street until they reached an old stone clock tower. The tower bell swayed loosely in the steeple far above.

"Now you have seen the state of our village you must begin to fathom the threat we face in this land," Magister Lunaris proclaimed once the group stopped.

"What could have done this?" Fletcher whispered in Gladius' ear, his apprehension apparent.

Easily overhearing Fletcher's whisper the Magister, Lunaris, answered his query. "The monster that did this we call 'The Wickerman' he resides in the nearby willow cemetery. Generations of our people have been buried there and now they are revived to act as his minions, ravaging our town and terrifying our citizens," Magister Lunaris explained glumly.

The faces of the other dark elves matched his despair. "We are prepared to swear fealty to the crown of Myst City if you will help us rid our lands of this evil," Magister Lunaris promised.

Gladius stepped forward and slipped his helmet on, "Let's do this!" he declared which was followed by an erupting cheer. He still couldn't believe he was working with these deserters.

The wind fell silent as Gladius and Fletcher reached the cemetery with the small handful of dark elves Darkwoods Outpost could spare.

The world around them lulled as they crossed the iron gates at the entrance, the dark elves tip-toed nervously behind, careful to not make a sound. The willow trees dotted around the cemetery were hunched over, swaying silently. The gravestones stood like stone teeth from the mouth of the graveyard grounds. This was the calm before the storm.

All of a sudden the heavy iron gates slammed shut with a loud rattling bang, startling everyone. The group spun around to see that they had been locked in.

The tall barbed fence offered no alternate exit. The iron bars had become their prison. One of the dark elves ran up to the gates shaking it frantically before crying out and falling to his knees defeated.

"We're all going to die!" wailed another of the dark elves. Gladius who was standing next to him struck him across the face stopping him silent.

"This only ensures we will achieve what we set out here to do," he barked.

All around the wind began to pick up. The willows pulsed and the brittle brown grass rustled. The moon became the witness to the oncoming carnage.

"Get ready everyone!" issued Fletcher as he loaded his bow with a long silver arrow and tensed the string, looking around with one eye closed and the other keen.

Gladius drew his sword and stood silently, his red cape fluttered behind him in the gale. The dark elves mimicked his defensive stance and held out their swords. Fletcher's plume and the dark elves' long hair flickered viciously in the strong wind.

The nearest gravestone cracked and toppled over; the ground beneath them began shaking. A bead of sweat ran down Gladius' face, luckily concealed under his helmet.

The first rotted hand burst out of the ground grabbing one of the dark elf's ankles.

"Ah!" the dark elf yelped struggling hysterically.

"Over there!" instructed Gladius pointing at another zombie pulling itself up with its boney arms stripped of flesh.

The grotesque decayed face was crawling with maggots, it was withered to the point that it was impossible to tell if it was an elf or a human in life.

The empty eye sockets lay fixed on Fletcher. Fletcher launched an arrow straight into the zombie's brittle forearm, shattering its single remaining bone. It fell to the side and it struggled to surface with one arm.

This victory seemed futile considering zombies were raising everywhere, groaning and gurgling. A crowd of them descended on the dark elves despite them swinging their swords wildly. Eventually they were engulfed by the mob and fell under a pile of them.

Their screams were replaced by the gurgling and munching noises of the zombies furiously feasting on them. Gladius and Fletcher continued knocking one zombie after another down. Gladius decapitated them left and right but it was fruitless—they continued shambling on, the broken bodies relentless.

"Look out!" called out Gladius as a zombie lunged at Fletcher's back. Gladius drew a dagger from his ankle and whipped it straight into the zombie's spine knocking it flat.

"Thanks!" Fletcher replied with a sigh of relief. Gladius acknowledged with a nod.

The graveyard was teeming with undead now; the earth was littered with open pits and exposed graves. It didn't seem to matter where or how the zombies were struck, they continued forth undaunted, shambling at a snail's pace. The gurgling and moaning got louder and louder as the zombies anticipated their next meal—the two heroes.

The dark elves' corpses were still being picked and chewed at by the frenzied zombies, their faces red with blood.

"Our weapons aren't working, we need iron!" Gladius declared between decapitating and kicking away zombies.

"Then we transmute!" replied Fletcher, eager to try out the augmentations Astralode had given them for such an occasion. He had inscribed symbols of metallic transmutation on their quiver and sheath.

The white light of a transmutation poured out of Fletcher's quiver as the etching on it activated. His arrows reformed themselves into sanctified iron in an instant. Gladius did likewise, returning his sword to its sheath, transmuting it to iron before wielding it once more.

In one fell swoop Gladius halved the nearest zombie; it sizzled and bubbled as it fell, melting into the ground leaving only browned bones.

"Much better!" grinned Gladius as he defeated another. Fletcher's arrows struck the undead enemies in their chests exploding them into lifeless piles of bones.

Before long, the graveyard was empty, littered only with the browned bones of the fallen undead. The victorious heroes hunched as they caught their breath, smiles of relief on their faces.

"We still haven't seen any sign of The Wickerman," Gladius panted, his concern matched only by his fatigue.

"Over there!" Fletcher pointed back to Darkwoods Outpost, thick smoke rose above the clearing, clouding over the moon. Dull screams echoed through the night sky.

"We have to break down this gate and get back there!" Gladius nodded to Fletcher who instantly knew the plan. The two of them charged the gate crashing into it and sending it flying off its rusted hinges. They sped off into the woods finally emerging in the clearing around the outpost.

Crimson flames lit up the night sky.

Seeing the flames, memories The Capital under siege by Greed's armies returned to Gladius in a flash.

He was once again standing amongst the carnage in The Capital watching the terrible events once more. Trolls and goblins ran around joyously with torches igniting one building after another. Others were fighting with the city guards, overpowering them with their immense clubs and maces.

Greed's siege engines had broken through the walls. Legions of abominations of every kind poured into the city. Greed watched from his throne elevated by four ogre load-bearers.

A look of sadistic amusement colored Greed's face, lit up by the roaring flames. His demonic visage was awash in the delight of the brutality surrounding him. The night was illuminated by the flames and its ambience was the screams of women and children echoing everywhere. Those screams still haunted Gladius in his waking hours.

Greed's Consul: Affluence was ordering the various loyalists to show no mercy, women and children were being killed en mass and once the last of the city guards fell only the scattered soldiers of the ally cities remained.

The small militia detachments of Myst City, Sunrise City, and Plateau City were too few in number to curb the invasion of Greed's legions.

One particular loyalist of Greed was a necromancer, Seth; his familiars were butchering the innocent around him.

Gladius watched as the younger version of him sliced and diced the vile familiars of Seth, and engaged the necromancer in armed combat.

Seth looked very similar to Umbra, though far older, but they shared much of the same features. His powers were very different. There was definitely a connection between him and Umbra, reason enough that Gladius was still suspicious of Umbra.

As the younger Gladius swung his sword wildly at Seth, he grew increasingly fatigued. Seth was sapping his strength with his foul magic. Every blow the sorcerer landed weakened Gladius further. Eventually Gladius caved to his knees, he didn't stand a chance, and his face was littered with scars from Seth's dagger. Blood dripped over his eyes making it even harder to fight this impossible battle.

Gladius collapsed onto his back, utterly defeated as he awaited the necromancer Seth to deal the final blow. His eyes closed, he waited.

"Assemble!" a voice rang out followed by a horn blast, Gladius watched as Seth walked away flashing a saddened glance at him as he left. That gaze lingered with him; it wasn't a look of malice, but one of regret and shame.

The last thing he remembered was being carried out by some retreating Myst City soldiers as he was losing consciousness. The battle was over for him and he would be bed-ridden for months to follow.

No. He thought. *That was no battle, it was a massacre!*

"Are you coming boss?" echoed Fletcher's voice hazily.

Gladius snapped back to reality to see Fletcher staring at him with a concerned look on his face.

"We have to get back to Darkwoods Outpost!" he insisted. "Err . . . Are you okay, boss?" Fletcher added.

"Of course, let's go!" Gladius agreed, dismissively.

TWENTY EIGHT

UMBRA AND MARIN CONTINUED onwards. They descended the final mountain path and came into view of the hellish wasteland of The Lava Fields.

The air around them was fouled by the rising smoke of numerous geysers around them. The floor was dusted, dry magma. Nothing seemed to grow, everything looked scorched.

Some of the cracks were exposed, revealing rivers of fire flowing like veins under the seemingly dead landscape. Their view ahead was rippled from the rising heat.

"Just over the peaks on the far side," Marin instructed, breaking the silence.

Umbra's cloak had been removed and slung over his shoulder, leaving only his simple grey clothes, discolored with sweat and dust. His hair was damp from fatigue and stuck to his forehead.

"We should probably keep moving. Once that slayer is free she will hunt us down. We should get as much distance from her as possible . . ." he looked back at Marin. She was glowing with a silvery-blue aura and stood in the center of a hydromantic array.

Umbra eyeballed her, about to speak when she raised a finger to her mouth to shush him. Then with her arms outstretched, the array began to spin faster and faster. Steam rose up from the ground and enshrouded her, whirling with the array. The large cloud rose up to conceal her until it finally dissipated, revealing Marin hunched over and panting, gripping her staff like a feeble old lady.

Umbra looked at her feet to notice a dozen vials of water, still glowing from their conjuring.

He ran to grab her as she collapsed and raised a bottle to her parched lips, while stroking her hair affectionately. Once the cool water passed her lips, life sprung into her face and she jumped to her feet.

"Where are we?" inquired Umbra between huge gulps of water.

"We have just entered The Lava Fields. I used the vapor around us to form that water. We will need it, this part of the trip can get pretty rough, Umbra," Marin explained looking at him with a smile on her face as he gulped the water.

So there the two sorcerers walked, slowed by the searing heat, and daunted by the Dead Landscape. Umbra wondered if they were even going in the right direction, the dust cloud in the distance concealed the horizon.

Marin seemed sure of their course so he said nothing and continued forth towards the unknown. For hours they walked, or rather stumbled until something other than dust and rock appeared through the dust-cloud horizon.

Rising peaks, and a giant crevasse that glowed red from the molten hell-fires below; the crevasse stretched as far as the eye could see in either direction. They had to cross it; there was no way around it.

A red banner flapping in the wind caught Umbra's attention, marked with a skull surrounded by fire.

"I was hoping we wouldn't have to deal with the molten-core bandits, this is very bad," Marin stuttered, her anxiety apparent. "They will kill us on sight; they are extremely territorial, and violent."

"We can try sneaking through I suppose," Marin suggested looking at Umbra, trying to conceal her angst.

The moon shone overhead. "I think we should wait until later hours, we can hopefully sneak by undetected as the guards turn in," said Umbra. "My powers are much stronger should we have to fight our way through," he gloated.

"Freeze scum!" ordered four Myst City guards patrolling to the north of the city.

They had stumbled upon Micah and Vlad heading north in the Werewolf Woods to find the Demon, Lust. The guards lowered their pikes, pointing their spear-points at the two black-clad perpetrators.

Micah continued walking away casually, his expression lacked concern and his sword hung over his shoulder, Vlad nervously walking behind him. Vlad's power was minimal in the light of day; he was hesitant to engage the guards.

"I said freeze!" demanded one guard. Micah stopped abruptly, but not out of fear.

The wind in the trees made them rustle; they suddenly stopped dead, almost like the holding their breath. The necromancer and his companion turned to them and looked menacingly at the guards.

The guards shuffled nervously upon realizing who they had provoked.

"Just walk away" warned Micah casually. Vlad nodded with an evil grin across his face, his fangs were revealed. The guards grunted with contempt.

"You die, here, today scum," they affirmed, hiding their fear.

"Don't say we didn't warn you," Micah sighed, his sword lighting up.

Micah and Vlad ran towards the guards, Micah was much faster than the vampire, being was the first to draw blood with a quick, clean kill. The guard didn't even have time to react as the sword penetrated his neck. A look of horror was frozen on his face as he dropped lifelessly to the floor. The sword, almost as if savoring the blood illuminated a fierce red.

"You left me no choice" Micah sighed, looking down at the fallen guard. He stepped on the guard's helmet to extract his blade and held it over his head. However he hesitated, deciding against taking the guard's soul.

Vlad was already chewing fiercely on one of the other guards. He was obviously hungry judging by his frantic bloodlust.

"Vampire, stop! We made our point," Micah snapped, disgusted by the vampire's feeding frenzy.

Vlad leant up wiping his bloodied face with his sleeve. The other guards had already started running, almost tripping over each other in their desperation.

Vlad looked over at Micah, "should we chase them?" he inquired.

"Let them go, we'll be long gone before they return with reinforcements," Micah assured him as he wiped down his blade with his cape.

He held up the sword to examine it, various swirling white souls permeated through it's blade including his—the grey-colored one. This was only a fraction of his soul. The rest lay in its natural vessel and that's where he intended it to remain. Micah could hear a cold, deep breath as he fixated on the swords blade. He scowled.

Soon Umbra would face justice at the edge of the blade.

"I'm hungry, I won't last if I don't feed," protested Vlad, watching the remaining two guards flee off into the woods.

"Fine, eat this one," Micah sighed with an unusual lack of concern. He kicked the lifeless guard he had killed towards Vlad.

What's happening to me?

Vlad fed furiously on the fallen soldier without uttering a word.

"Disgusting," Micah grumbled as he watched Vlad chewing furiously with hunger.

Micah looked down at his blood-spattered hands.

How much more blood will have to be spilled?

TWENTY NINE

GLADIUS AND FLETCHER SPED off down a shallow hill through a long, narrow plot of dead cornfields that lined the northern edge of the outpost.

They didn't have time to give any of the peculiar scarecrows a second glance. They had to hurry towards the fires of Darkwoods Outpost. The entire forest was lit up like the sun.

It's time these fires were doused. Gladius resolved.

Zombies swarmed the burning town, undaunted by the guards. The dark elves were falling by the dozen as the undead horde rampaged, hacking down innocent civilians with their rusted weapons.

Magister Lunaris, the leader of the dark elves issued orders to his troops assembled near the smoldering town hall. "Keep together! Archers to the rear; stay in formation!" he ordered. The dark elves saluted in unison.

The few surviving citizens fled in every direction, screaming at the top of their lungs. The chaos spread like a plague, the town would soon fall. Gladius and Fletcher arrived on the scene, hacking and piercing zombies as they went.

"Where's The Wickerman?" Gladius demanded, looking intensely at the Magister as he arrived on the scene.

"He's moved into the trade district!" one of the dark elves explained, shifting nervously near the front of the formation.

"Let's go Fletcher!"

"Sure thing, boss!" replied Fletcher, not halting his flurry of arrows.

The two sped off in the direction of the fiercest flames.

And there he was, The Wickerman, a monstrous combination of scarecrow and demon.

His limbs were stitched with straw poking out of the seams, he wore ragged clothes and had a woven straw hat pulled down over his eyes. Jet black wings were folded behind his back. He pointed towards the nearest house commanding his zombies to torch it.

I guess these zombies aren't as stupid as they appear, Gladius thought to himself, as he watched the shambling undead carrying torches over to the building.

"Spare none!" hissed The Wickerman. He turned to notice the two heroes standing at the ready, his head cocked to the side with a curious stare.

"Your time is up, Wickerman!" yelled Fletcher, his voice dampened by the crackling flames.

"Who are these fools?" The Wickerman inquired. He felt no threat by these non-elf interlopers despite their fearlessness.

Fletcher released an arrow into flight, piercing The Wickerman in the shoulder. "That almost tickled," mocked The Wickerman as he pulled out the arrow and snapped it in two with one hand.

Straw poked out of his wound, there was no blood. Fletcher was dumbstruck.

Umbra jumped to his feet and backed away from the smoke plume. "Could it be?" Umbra began.

He knew exactly what to expect before it even appeared.

Belphagor! The hulking red demon and holder of contracts was once again before him, arms crossed and steaming sulfurous breath.

"What do you want?! I still have eleven months!" Umbra demanded angrily.

The demon smiled coyly, enraging Umbra further.

"Tell me what you want before I lose my patience!" Umbra threatened, clutching his hand, his scar burning brightly.

"We have plans for you Umbra," the demon explained ominously.

Umbra had heard enough, he swirled his hand until a black orb formed, and reached back to cast it at the demon.

Undaunted, the demon narrowed his eyes. Umbra howled in pain as his scar ignited. Umbra's spell dissipated as he dropped to the floor wrenching in agony, stirring up ash as he smothered the flame.

"That scar I gave you is imbued with power," said the demon, making steps towards Umbra. He hovered above the lava effortlessly, walking until he stood on the burnt shore. He towered over Umbra, his dead eyes piercing the young necromancer's mind.

"Like I said, you're around because we have plans for you," the demon grinned evilly.

He reached his down and grabbed Umbra's scarred hand. The nauseating smell of burning flesh filled Umbra's nostrils as the demon squeezed, Umbra's veins blackened, becoming visible all over his body. He struggled in vain to wriggle out of the demon's grasp. The demon finally released his hand as the veins faded. Umbra's head ached as his heartbeat pounded in his ears like a drum.

"Your veins flow with the corruption of a demon, I'm just helping you along" Belphagor jested.

"Enjoy your power, I'll be seeing you soon," the demon echoed as he vanished. The only remnant of the demon's presence was a sulfurous stench lingering in the air.

Umbra looked down at his hand, his nails were blackened and sharp and his body surrounded by a faint black aura. The markings had spread across his entire body. Strange purple symbols and swirled burns covered him now. He couldn't bear to look at them; the deafening beat of his heart rang in his ears.

My veins flow with the corruption of a demon? Am I a . . .? He contemplated.

No! He affirmed. The markings faded once he calmed himself down.

He quietly snuck back to where Marin lay hoping not to wake her. It wouldn't be long until they had the full cover of night. As he saw the gulley, he froze in horror. She was gone!

He ran over to the small gulley frantically and examined the floor. It was still damp; she had struggled and had been taken off somewhere.

A small red armband lay torn on the floor; it had the emblem of the molten-core bandits. Looking toward their camp by the massive lava-crevasse to the east he knew that's where he had to go.

I hope Marin is still alive.

He pulled his black robe on and ran towards the glowing crevasse far off.

"Marin, I'm coming!" he yelled.

"I'm finally free!" cheered Robyn. Her smile instantly turned into a searing frown. "I'll gut that necromancer when I get my hands on him," she scowled.

She cracked her knuckles and sprinted down the rocky mountain path towards The Lava Fields.

I can't believe I let that amateur trap me like that!

She hated herself for that single mistake in her battle. Those few moments of broken concentration with Umbra had done her in. She was determined to make him pay.

As she continued running down the mountain trail she reminisced of her past. She remembered the day she decided to become a slayer.

Once again The Capital was burning. All those years back she was only a young girl when the city was under siege by Greed's army. His legions had breached the walls and poured into the streets, dragging civilians out onto the lanes, butchering them mercilessly.

Greed's loyalists were there too. One loyalist in particular she remembered clearest. It still boiled her blood when she remembered him. She could never forget such a heartless monster!

The necromancer, Seth! That runt, Umbra's father!

Her hatred for him was what drove her and it was on that day when her family was taken away from her that she decided to become a slayer.

Her family had hidden away in the cellar under their modest house, tormented by the screams of their friends and neighbors. One of Seth's monstrous familiars had heard their heavy breathing and torn the cellar doors off their hinges, exposing them to the carnage.

She could only look on in horror as they dragged her parents out onto the street, dropping them at their master's feet. She saw Seth kill each of them, using his foul magic to absorb their souls.

She had screamed at the top of her lungs when he turned his attention to her, his cold expressionless face still haunted her.

Before Seth could make a move he was intercepted by a swordsman clad in silver armor and a red cape. He too like the hydromancer companion of Umbra bore the symbol of the Golden Sun. The swordsman had jumped into the fray to duel the evil sorcerer.

Robyn fled at that point, tears streaming down her face. She stumbled upon a retreating soldier who dragged her from that nightmarish battle.

Later on she was left at an orphanage, where she stayed until old enough to leave. Once she left the orphanage she was employed as a laborer but was determined that one day she would be the best slayer in the land.

She intended to make Seth pay for his crimes, but for now she could only do the next best thing—punish his son.

Her desire for revenge, and justice burned brighter than the flames of The Capital.

Umbra! He hissed under her breath. *I will find you!* She promised herself.

THIRTY

"**G**ENERAL, WE ARE NEARING the edge of the Wetlands," a troll informed, before falling back to formation in the Troll division.

"Send a goblin forward!" War Chief Groll ordered from atop his snarling hell-steed. "We need to scout ahead."

A goblin obediently ran to the front of the lines, his loosely fitting iron armor clanked as he ran.

Their straight marching trail through the swamp had left a widened path of destruction, plants were crushed, and trees hacked down. They had torn through, even nearby animals were slaughtered needlessly.

The wildlife of the Wetlands sighed in relief as the battalion neared the exit to their lands. The chirping and other noises of the swamp were hushed and quiet as the interlopers marched onwards.

A single black raven sailed through the humid fog of the canopy and landed on War Chief Groll's shoulder.

"What is it, messenger?" he inquired as the raven looked at him. The raven shifted on his shoulder and bent over to whisper in his ear.

Perfect! He thought. "We head to Ferus Town on the outskirts immediately!"

"Pick up the pace!" he bellowed.

The skeletons automatically upped their speed, word spread through the ranks and the exhausted warriors struggled to move faster. One of the goblins collapsed in the mucky trail and was ignored by the marching legion until he reached War Chief Groll's sights.

He eyeballed him sternly. "Get to your feet, peon!" he demanded. The goblin struggled to breathe; sweat ran down his green-tinted body. Struggling to elevate himself he collapsed once more.

War Chief Groll nodded to the nearest troll soldier. Without hesitation the troll smashed the helpless goblin's skull open with a swing of his immense cudgel.

The march didn't even react as they left his broken body to rot in the dank, humid wetland trail.

All of a sudden a sharpened projectile sailed through the air, impaling itself into one of the goblins, who collapsed with a yelp. The troops automatically assumed a defensive formation, raising their shields. Nervous chatter ensued as they waited.

"Who dares?" demanded War Chief Groll from atop his steed.

A large Leshy stepped forward, a hulking figure with skin like bark and a beard of moss. The troops stood still in fear as many more Leshy stepped forward. The battalion was surrounded!

"Conjuror Mathias, our master, demands that you leave this place immediately without resistance!" the first Leshy boomed.

"We are here on command from Lord Greed, and you are in our way!" declared War Chief Groll. The General issued the order for the goblin archers to fire. The trolls and skeletons grinned as they preened their weapons to hack and slash.

The Leshy crowd extended long vines from their hands, impaling many of the swordsmen who rushed them. The goblins lit their arrows and released a volley into the fray. The Leshy who were struck erupted in flame yet continued their attack.

Eventually the enflamed Leshy collapsed into a heaps of charcoal and the rest were hacked down.

"It looks like we have firewood now, boys!" War Chief Groll smirked dismounting his hell-steed to examine their charred remains.

"Hack down the trees, before we leave we'll torch this dump!" He laughed manically as his horde cheered.

"Allazh, Mallaki, Aruuum," Magister Lunaris and his sorcerers chanted in harmony.

They were almost drowned out by the crackling flames of Darkwoods Outpost.

Gladius and Fletcher rushed The Wickerman with weapons drawn. He flapped his bat-like wings, lifting himself slightly off the ground and pelting them with a gust of wind.

Leaning into the wind and pacing forwards, the heroes were determined to apprehend this fiend. Before they could get closer The Wickerman lunged through the air with his hand-scythes and chopped Gladius' sword in two. Gladius face was frozen in shock as he held the stump of a sword.

"The next time it will be your head!" the demonic scarecrow threatened, staring Gladius down with an evil grin.

The Wikerman's minions were tearing apart the sorcerers one by one; their chant was becoming quieter with each death.

The Wickerman swooped in for the final blow on Gladius. The veteran swordsman swung with a concealed katana, quickly chopping the Wickerman's arm. It slid straight through, amputating it. Straw fell out of the opening scattering on Gladius.

The straw encircled him like a cyclone. He covered his eyes, coughing wildly. Fletcher grabbed the fallen hand-scythe and dashed towards The Wickerman with it.

The ground suddenly lit up beneath Fletcher's feet and his quiver radiated purple light.

"Fire an arrow and deal the final blow, Archer!" Magister Lunaris bellowed swatting the zombies off him.

Fletcher whipped out his bow and launched a glowing purple arrow at The Wickerman; the arrow struck the fiend in the forehead erupting with a burst of purple light.

A circle formed around The Wickerman, swirling wildly before erupting in an immense shockwave. The zombies all over town collapsed to the ground, melting like ice in a hearth.

The swirling straw around Gladius dissipated leaving him hunched over and coughing.

The lifeless husk of the demonic fiend lay limp on the spot he had been struck, his wings frozen in stone and ragged clothes crumbling.

"It's over," Fletcher sighed as he helped Gladius to his feet.

Gladius looked down at the stump of a sword he held in his off-hand and tossed it to the ground.

"Good job, Fletcher," he smiled as Magister Lunaris walked over to praise them.

"The least we can do now is to offer our loyalty to the former alliance. We'll stand by you when you need us," the Magister promised, bowing in respect.

"There will be a battle soon when we'll need you, the wizard Astralode will contact you," Gladius replied with a respectful bow.

"When that day comes I will fight beside you as a brother. We owe our lives to you, heroes," the Magister nodded. The other dark elves genuflected.

The two victorious heroes handed Magister Lunaris one of the scrying orbs given to them by Astralode to contact him. Calling their horses, they turned west to continue their journey.

THIRTY ONE

ACK AT THE RUINS of The Capital, the demon lord Greed sat perched on his usurped throne. He was clad in the late king's crown jewels. He rolled a diamond-studded gold scepter in his hand being careful not to scratch it with his razor-sharp talons.

His raven scouts had informed him that Micah had changed course and was heading north to the Lust's temple in The Dying Lands.

He slammed his fist down in frustration. The advisors in the chamber jumped, startled by the immense noise.

"Not to worry, my lord, the boy is taking a small detour, but his goal remains the same," assured Affluence, the lesser demon and chief advisor.

"What if Lust makes him stronger than Umbra?" Greed inquired, his anger still fuming.

"The contract demon has already awoken much of Umbra's dark power. He'll still be stronger, and once Micah dies his soul will be trapped in that sword. Umbra will surely take the sword and we'll have two souls for the price of one!" Affluence grinned.

"Minion! Go fetch my scrying orb!" Greed demanded. The nearest skeleton soldier standing at his side marched off to get it.

The old stone chamber fell silent once again as a satyr scout emerged from the hallway, sprinting down the red carpet towards Greed.

"A message from Demon Overlord, Wrath!" the satyr announced unrolling a scroll.

Greed was always disgusted by the way Wrath introduced himself in messages. He sighed, sitting back down on his throne, his many jewels jingled as he shifted in his seat.

"Go ahead, messenger!" he ordered. The satyr unrolled the scroll and took a deep breath. Affluence looked intently at him, standing in absolute silence eager to hear the news.

"To my subject, Lord Greed I request an update from Lord Apathy immediately," the satyr recited. Greed knew that Wrath hated Apathy for his recklessness, refusing to contact him directly. Apathy would go on a killing spree then hibernate for years; he acted too independently for Wrath's liking.

The satyr bowed and handed the scroll to Affluence, walking over to sit in the pews against the back wall.

"What shall we say, my lord?" Affluence inquired.

"Tell him that Apathy has messed up again and Micah is off course," he grunted.

He too, hated using Apathy in his plans, he was erratic.

Affluence quickly scribbled the message down on a blank scroll on the map-board table. He handed it to the eager satyr who sped off to The Temple of the Damned to return to his master.

Affluence looked down at the magical map etched in the stone; a red marker indicated any demonic presence. They were using this to follow the movements of Umbra.

"Send a phantom horseman to Lust's temple and have him 'lose' his steed in the battle. We need to hurry Micah along before Umbra's time runs out," Affluence affirmed. "It'll be much harder to retrieve his soul from the underworld than from the Sword of Twilight."

"Not to worry, once his time expires the soul will be contained within the sword if he has it in his possession," Greed explained, rolling a gem in his hands before tossing it onto his huge treasure hoard.

"If Umbra arrives here before his time expires, it'll be to steal the Spear of Destiny and we'll simply take his soul in our own way," Greed added.

He knew that he hadn't been told of the whole plan by Wrath. Wrath never trusted him with all the information, something was always secretive.

"You heard our master!" Affluence barked.

One of the advisors sped off down the carpeted chamber. The skeleton soldier returned and handed the scrying orb to Greed.

The advisor descended the winding stone staircase to the torture chamber; burning blue torches lit the advisors path.

The torturer, Malus, a pestilence sorcerer turned away from his labor to address the advisor.

His white skin was withered and wrinkled, his glowing red eyes lit up. He was a shade, an entity created when a sorcerer sells their soul for immortality and gives into their evil urges, becoming a twisted abomination. Anything human in Malus was long gone.

Screams echoed throughout the torture chamber. The old stone walls flickered from the dim torches dotted around the room. Every manner of torture device littered the chamber. It was a morbid shrine of agony.

Iron-shackled victims hung upside-down on the wall, most of them dead. The few living were tattered and brutalized, barely recognizable in their miserable state.

The living victims pleaded to die; their cries were like music to Malus' ears.

Malus stepped back from the wooden rack where he was flame-branding a dark-haired young woman. Goblins in black hoods were hot-pokering her. She screamed in agony until eventually blacking out.

One of the goblins ran to grab some cold water to wake her up so they could continue.

"What can I do for you?" Malus inquired with a hissing voice.

"Greed ordered we unleash a phantom horseman to hurry the sorcerer, Micah, to Lust's temple immediately. Be sure it's a weaker one, and the horse is fast," the advisor issued.

"You heard the demon!" Malus barked to the nearest goblin. The hooded goblin ran off excitedly to gather the cursed skull reagent.

He returned with a blackened skull and placed it in his master's hands. Malus clutched the skull tightly; it lit up an eerie blue. Suddenly a black portal opened and a shadowy horseman galloped into view. The rider was devoid of anything above his neck, there was no head on this specter.

The phantom horse snarled and grunted, its figure shimmered, and it resembled more a shadow than a living being.

Malus tossed the skull to the phantom rider that placed it on its bare neck. The skull burst into blue flame, hovering above the figure.

"Very impressive, sorcerer!" the advisor beamed with an evil grin.

Malus issued the phantom rider his orders and watched it run through another open black portal, leaving behind only a wisp of black mist.

"I love my job," Malus grinned with sadistic pleasure as he turned back to the victim on the rack and extracted a hot brand. "Now it's time for us to continue our little conversation."

THIRTY TWO

MICAH AND VLAD PRESSED forward towards the Dying Lands barely speaking a word to each other.

The ground was a dead grey and dotted with charred skeletons and ruined buildings. The sky was clouded over and darkened. There was no moon in view and strange noises echoed all around.

"How far is it to this temple?" Micah inquired impatiently.

Vlad hadn't said a word in hours and was lost in thought.

Will he kill me when I'm not useful anymore?

He looked at Micah cautiously.

"The temple should be coming up soon, but we must be careful not to stray off the trail or we'll end up in the ruins of The Capital," Vlad explained, trying to hide his anxiety.

Micah eyed him curiously. He could sense Vlad's growing suspicions.

"What's in those ruins that we should be afraid of?" he asked, halting in his tracks. Vlad stopped and turned to him.

"The demon Greed lives there with his immense army, and he is not fond of outsiders," Vlad explained.

Before Micah could respond he stopped himself. A loud battle cry was heard close by.

Vlad grabbed Micah's hand and ducked behind a ruined wall. He shushed him, pointing through a small peep-hole in the stone.

Micah looked through the opening to see a large shadowy figure on horseback. The entire rider and horse resembled a shimmering shadow, only the rider's head was a blue flaming skull. The horse grunted as the rider scanned around before dismounting.

As he walked closer, Micah's sword began glowing red. He quickly covered it over with his black cloak, but it got brighter and was just as visible. The rider looked directly at the wall where Micah and Vlad were hiding.

"He knows we're here!" Vlad yelled as he jumped out from behind the crumbled wall. Their only chance was to attack together.

"I don't sense much power in it," Micah reassured Vlad. The phantom horseman looked directly at Micah and drew an iron mace also wrapped in that strange eerie fire.

Vlad tried to pull the weapon to his hand with his magic but it did nothing. He was nowhere near as strong as Lydia was.

Micah stormed towards the rider, impaling him with his red glowing sword. The phantom dropped and immediately evaporated.

"That was . . . easy," Micah muttered in a state of surprise. Vlad looked at him with bewilderment.

"It was almost like it threw the fight," Vlad stuttered. *That seemed a little too easy* he worried.

Micah looked up to see the shadowy horse standing obediently a few feet away. "Should we use the horse?" Vlad inquired.

"The faster the better I say!" Micah beamed, barely able to believe his luck.

Micah leapt onto the shadowy horse and Vlad joined him. He whipped the horse's reins and it sped off down the dusty trail. The wind blasted their faces from the sheer speed of their mount.

Micah couldn't believe his good fortune. He could get to Lust's temple and catch up to Umbra easily now.

Nearby in the ruins of The Capital, Greed sat intently on his throne. The echoes of the night lulled as his advisors convened.

"Perfect!" Greed grinned, leaning over his crystal scrying orb. His plan had worked—Micah had taken the phantom horse from their decoy soldier.

His advisors were gathered around the map table discussing their next move.

"My liege, what do we do now?" Affluence inquired. He looked at Greed expectantly.

"Simple. All we have to do now is wait," Greed grinned. He looked down at a gem ring on his finger and gawked vainly at his reflection.

"Soon, soon we will have exactly what we want," he rolled the gem in his claws and reminisced.

Dominance!

Lost in thought, he was once again standing on the final battlefield of the Twilight Wars. He stood behind Wrath, clad in a gold breastplate, his hulking figure barely contained in it. Greed's own armor was far more decorative, adorned with the riches he had plundered; his black scales shimmered in the sunlight. He fidgeted with his scimitar in its holster, eager to start the fight.

Clouds began gathering over the battlefield, the sky was darkening. The ranks of trolls, ogres, golems, and all matter of loyalist monsters grunted in anticipation.

The call rang out and the battle began, the rain-washed field became a tangled chaos of swords and arrows within seconds.

Greed hammered armored elves with his mace, light-headed with euphoria. He stomped on an injured soldier lying on the ground. The man crunched under his hoof.

He loved seeing all of the misery and suffering. He relished the spoils from each battle: the shiny jeweled weapons, territory; he was living a dream he thought would never end.

The battle had continued for hours, casualties on either side were piling up. The skies seemed to rain red with blood, the field was awash in it.

Word circulated that the demon lords were being sealed, Greed didn't believe, this nor would he let it distract him from the slaughter.

No mortal can kill a demon lord! He had firmly believed.

He looked atop the overlooking cliffs. His mistress, Zuul was perched on the end of her seat. *Why was she so anxious?* He wondered.

The Grand Alliance soldiers around him were beaten and broken. He wandered casually towards another chaotic skirmish, his jeweled mace at the ready.

Before he got there he felt a sharp pain in his back, he had been speared by a swordsman's javelin. The swordsman wore silver armor and had a flowing black beard. He bore a strong resemblance to the knight of Myst City, Gladius, but this was centuries prior.

Greed had been around long enough to realize that heroes like that were often reincarnated.

He had fought this soldier who had adeptly clipped Greed's shins and slowed him down immensely.

The swordsman had leapt out of the fray just before Greed was enveloped in a purple illumination; a young Astralode had conjured a binding array around him.

The last thing Greed remembered before blacking out was the blinding purple light engulfing him.

The next time he awoke he was standing in The Temple of the Damned surrounded by Wrath's sorcerers. His other brethren were also released from their prisons.

Wrath had gathered them together, informing them that Zuul had been sealed away. This news was received with mixed responses; Pride was actually elated at the prospect and made no effort to conceal his desire for power. Wrath had demanded that as second-in-command to Zuul, he was in charge. It wasn't long before the demon lords were squabbling over territory and leadership, eventually separating. Only he and Apathy remained loyal to Wrath.

Zuul had been defeated, sealed away in Pandora's Box. *The demon of the apocalypse defeated!* It didn't seem real. Wrath's only concern ever since was hunting down Pandora's Box.

THIRTY THREE

UMBRA SNUCK PAST THE sentry towers outlining the camp of the molten-core bandits', reaching an old wooden bridge. He was amazed by the bustling activity as he peered down below.

Glowing red lava flowed and cascaded through the giant crevasse. The rock walls were lined with platforms and walkways, red drakes flew around carrying buckets of lava. Many ogre guards patrolled the camp.

What are they up to? Umbra wondered.

He saw a basket and pulley system and leapt into it, lowering himself slowly into the hell-fires below.

The various ogres patrolling nearby were clad in red emblem-covered tunics, carrying war hammers. He tied off the pulley and dropped silently onto a canopy covering a platform.

"What you think master wants with slave?" one of the nearby ogres asked the other.

Umbra peered over the edge.

"I don't know," answered the other guard scratching his bald head.

Who is their master? Umbra wondered as he continued to spy.

"Well, we can go down to the slave pens and see her. She is pretty," one ogre suggested.

"No stupid, we guard here!" the other one grunted, clubbing him on the head with his fist.

Umbra clenched his fist, his body lit up with strange purple symbols. He felt immense power pumping through his veins. He was ready to jump when suddenly he was struck with a vision.

He was looking through the eyes of somebody else, a battle was raging below. The carnage was unbelievable.

He recognized one of the warriors, Gladius! Their weapons and armor were very strange. The weapons were crudely made; their armor looked a lot heavier and unwieldy.

Am I seeing the distant past?

For some reason he really enjoyed watching the battlefield. The gore and carnage gave him a rush of euphoria. Strangely he wasn't in the fight, but merely watching it from above.

Purple lights lit up around the battlefield as immense roars were silenced.

They look like binding Circles!

The warrior that resembled Gladius was fighting a monster when a circle had lit up around it. He was hunched over and panting as the monster was engulfed in a flash of light leaving only a lifeless statue.

There was another familiar face. *Astralode!*

He looked a lot younger this time, around the age of a teenager. He was still wearing the same purple cloak he had seen him in.

How am I seeing this? Umbra wondered as the vision continued.

Suddenly, Umbra's view was raised almost like the watcher stood up and leapt off the cliff landing perfectly below. Surrounding soldiers from both sides stared up in fear.

With a single swing of a familiar obsidian sword, waves of soldiers were knocked away, tossed about like puppets. Arrows sailed towards him but were burnt up before they could even hit.

With the swing of his other hand another mass of soldiers were engulfed in a wave of shadows.

Why is Micah's sword in this vision? Umbra's concern grew further, not for himself but for his old friend. *What did we get ourselves tangled up in?*

Was this a demon? He thought. But the host was far too tall to be human. The arms crackled with a black flame and claws tipped each finger.

What is this? Umbra was panicking. *What's happening to me?!*

He snapped back to reality to realize he'd fallen off the canopy and landed right in front of the two guards.

The ogres looked down at him with stupid smiles. "We have another one now, master will be so pleased with us!" one exclaimed.

Umbra sighed in frustration. *Give me a break!*

THIRTY FOUR

THE OGRES LEANT DOWN to grab Umbra, without thinking about it he threw his hands up to cover himself.

His body lit up once more with the same strange, purple symbols. He waited and nothing happened.

Looking up he saw the two ogres frozen in pain. Their bodies were dissolving into dust. One tried to run but collapsed when his feet crumbled, falling to the floor.

Within seconds the two ogres where nothing but blackened ash.

Umbra looked at his hands. The strange symbols were glowing on his skin again. He felt energy surging through his body and an unnerving feeling. Despite the heat of the lava crevasse, he felt cold—empty, and immensely angry.

He wasn't even sure why he was so angry. Much to his surprise, standing on his feet felt much lighter.

He rolled up his sleeve; it was covered in those same symbols. Lifting up his shirt he saw the same thing. He was covered in head to toe with them.

"What is this?" he stammered. He had seen them somewhere before.

The Grimoire Demonus! There was a picture of a demon covered in them from head to toe!

Am I turning into one of them? His breath was panicked now.

How does Micah's sword fit into all of this?

He took several deep breaths and exhaled, blocking out the smell of lava and the noises all around. *I have to calm down! I'm here to save Marin!* The symbols on his body faded away slowly.

"As long as I don't get too worked-up Marin shouldn't see these markings."

I have to learn what these are. He promised himself. *Maybe Astralode will know.* He felt his pockets. The scrying orb was gone! *Damn! Marin must have it!*

He looked around, he was standing on a wooden boardwalk fastened the edge of the immense crevasse. It was a steep drop over the flimsy rope barriers into the fires below.

At the bottom was a gurgling lava flow, wooden boardwalks hugged the rock side. As far as he could tell, all of the guards were ogres like the ones he had just vaporized by accident.

Identical banners dotted the bridges, the red emblem of the bandits. Immense scarlet drakes flew past carrying large vats of molten lava with their talons, completely oblivious to Umbra as they continued their labors.

Partially armored ogres with huge clubs strolled along the wooden bridges.

A stone temple sculpted into the side of the rock caught his eye.

Is that where they're holding Marin?

He pulled his black hood over his face and tip-toed across the walkway towards it. The way was across a rickety bridge. In his haste he had left his pike behind where Marin had been abducted. He looked around for a weapon frantically, but there were only metal containers stacked against the wall.

"Oh well, this works," Umbra picked up one of the buckets, focusing in his mind of the weapon he wanted. The metal bucket glowed, swirling fluidly, reforming into a long dagger.

Perfect!

He gripped the dagger tightly, hoping to ambush the guards one by one.

The nearest sentry stood a few hundred meters away with his back turned. *Who's running this bandit clan? These ogres surely weren't.*

A shadow-step should work! He focused his mind, the world around him dulled. The grey-tone world he entered was like being in a hazy dream, devoid of color. It was a small trick he had picked up from Lady Crow.

He was standing in the shadow-world now. He'd been told repeatedly not to stay in this state for too long or it'd sap all of his strength, leaving him stranded in this weird half-death realm.

Umbra ran towards the nearby guard, leaping onto his back, dragging the blade across the ogre's neck. He muffled the ogre's cry with his hand and dropped him on the ground, stepping out of the shadow-world.

Sweat beaded on his head from the exertion of that other realm. He was only a vague shadow to onlookers when he used that little trick.

The next few guards noticed him emerge from the shadow-world and ran towards him, their heavy steps shaking the entire boardwalk.

"Let's see how you like a shadow-spear!" Umbra cried out, clenching his fist and making a swooping motion. His shadow shimmered beneath his feet, bursting forth as two sharpened shapes, impaling the two nearest guards.

Umbra stepped over the dead guards and continued on to the bridge. The next few guards were dealt with easily enough—Umbra had their own shadows attack them and strolled casually past.

This is so easy! Umbra was surprised how much stronger he had become; his scar glowed brightly under his glove, the light flickering through the seams. Not a single guard had managed to sound the alarm.

They all carried a horn on their belts, but none of them could get to it in time. However there was a strange feeling that he wasn't alone creeping down his spine even after the guards had been dealt with.

Umbra finally reached the doors to the temple. Stone gargoyles were perched on the roof looking down menacingly, their shadows flickered eerily.

Just in case they were living statues he decided to shadow-step past their view.

The inside of the temple was lit by burning braziers. Scary-looking statues were lined up against the walls and the clan's banners ran either side of the obsidian-colored floor.

There were no guards.

This must not be the right place.

Umbra turned around to leave when he heard the echo of a woman's scream.

"Marin!" He bolted down the hallway and up the carpeted stairs at the end of the chamber.

In his haste Umbra ran right in front of two armed ogre guards. They stood either side of a large stone door. Their grizzly expressions were partially covered by their bronze helmets.

Umbra raised his hand to attack, but the two ogres removed their crossed pikes from the doorway and ushered him in. Umbra walked through reluctantly.

The Contracted Soul

THIRTY FIVE

GLADIUS AND FLETCHER HAD finally reached the outskirts of Darkwoods. They halted their horses by a nearby wooden sign.

The shining twilight of open sky in the Golden Plains filled their view as they emerged from the forest.

Golden fields of wheat and tan-colored grass stretched as far as the nearest hillside. A small dusty road wound its way through the oddly unkempt crop fields.

"It says here we have to cross this plain, and then Squalor Mire. Plateau City should be on the coast," Fletcher explained. He sat atop his horse squinting as the brisk wind blew past carrying the smell of harvest.

"I really hope there's no more of those creepy scarecrows out here," Gladius grunted. He tensed the reins of his horse, speeding forward.

The two heroes galloped at full speed down the winding road, ready for what would await them.

The bright moonlight shone off Gladius' silver helmet as they closed in on the rising hillside. As they ascended the hillside and neared the top, a small settlement: Wheat Town came into view.

Old stone houses with thatched roofs, and cobble streets of the town were quite quaint. There was something missing however.

There wasn't a single soul to be seen.

Gladius and Fletcher's horses strolled slowly into the town the only noise heard was the wind. A dry fountain stood in the center of the town square.

"Hello!" Gladius called out into the empty town. His voice echoed through the empty streets. The town seemed to be abandoned.

"This doesn't seem right," Fletcher whispered to Gladius.

"Look over there!" Gladius pointed, dismounting his horse. He crouched down by a doorway to notice a small patch of blood; it was thick with what appeared to be slobber.

"I don't like this, boss, let's leave!" Fletcher called over to him from atop his horse.

Gladius held his ear to the door. Heavy breathing emanated from within. Gladius raised a finger to quiet Fletcher, who had dismounted to crouch behind him.

"What is it?" he whispered.

"There's somebody inside," Gladius whispered back. He stood up and carefully pushed the door open with a creak.

Umbra entered the illuminated chamber. It was circular with a sandy ring in the center; the room was filled with snarling ogres. The crowd of ogres stood around him, jeering at him. Through a window above he noticed the orange glow of the sun rising.

Pride stroked her hair and grabbed her head roughly.

"Let me tell you something about your little friend here," he grinned evilly. "Can you feel that evil force in him, my dear?" he inquired coyly.

"Uhh" Marin moaned her head hanging, her blonde hair covered her face.

Pride lifted her head in his hand and pointed her gaze at Umbra.

"You came all this way and plan to eradicate the demons when there was one right under your nose the whole time ready to sell you out!" Pride hissed into her ear.

"That's not true!" Umbra insisted.

"Keep watching, you'll see soon enough. The last thing you'll witness before you die is your friend revealing his true self," Pride's face darkened as he turned to Umbra "You can't fight it; you are destined to serve us!"

"I'm not going to let you turn me!" Umbra affirmed.

I can do this! I just can't give into this demonic power! Umbra's face beaded with sweat.

"You'll die for what you did to Marin!" he clenched his fist lightly. His scar lit up as he tried to hold back his full power.

"It will be my pleasure to turn you," Pride grinned. He clutched his hulking sword and loomed closer to Umbra.

THIRTY SIX

T HE DOOR OPENED SLOWLY with an eerie creaking noise. Gladius and Fletcher looked down. There was a trail of blood smeared across the wooden floor leading to the basement.

Gladius and Fletcher walked across the creaking wooden floorboards. They moved cautiously over to the basement door, carefully avoiding the blood. Gladius reached for the door-handle and turned it carefully. Fletcher shifted nervously as Gladius slowly opened the door.

The old wooden house was lit up by the now bright sunlight outside.

The old wooden staircase leading to the basement was still wet with blood. Gladius was about to descend the stairs when Fletcher tugged him back.

"I'll go. I've had plenty of practice sneaking up on people," he reminded Gladius.

Gladius nodded and stepped back.

Fletcher slid his bow over his shoulder and crept down the stairs.

The basement walls were covered in bloody smears and the air smelled stale.

He crouched to look around from the bottom of the stairs. He scanned the dim room; cobwebs covered the small windows blotting out the sunlight. There was a tall wardrobe in the corner; there were scratches on the stone floor—it had been moved recently.

"Hello?" Fletcher inquired, his bow raised and loaded. "I know you're behind there," he took a step forward.

"Don't, please, I'm sorry! We didn't have enough food this month. We can barely feed ourselves. You've killed everyone else, please just leave me alone," a voice called out.

"We aren't going to hurt you," Fletcher promised as he lowered his bow. "We are members of the Golden Sun." He motioned to Gladius to join him.

"We mean you no harm," Gladius insisted.

A young woman stepped out from behind the wardrobe. "You aren't with them," she sighed in relief. Her white apron was spattered with blood. Her eyes were lined with a tired expression.

"Are you hurt, ma'am?" Gladius queried reaching out his hand.

"The demon came, and his minions," she stuttered with a grim expression. "They demanded we give them our grain stocks . . . we didn't have enough," she began to cry.

"What was the demon's name?" Fletcher inquired softly, trying to soothe her.

They put their weapons away. "Do you know where they went?" Gladius added.

"It was Gluttony! Gluttony! He summoned locusts to ravage our town, and then his men collected the survivors to be taken for his next meal!" she cried out. Tears poured down her face.

"We'll slay that demon and rescue your village! Where is he?" Gladius insisted.

"To the north; he lives in a fort atop the tallest hill around, but his guards are everywhere," she explained tearfully.

She collapsed into a fetal position and began rocking back and forth. "Everywhere, they are everywhere," she whispered. She had clearly lost her wits.

"Ma'am?"

"Everywhere. Everywhere."

Gladius and Fletcher looked at each other. "We'll find your demon and give him what he deserves!" Gladius promised sternly.

"Everywhere. Everywhere."

The two heroes left the woman in the basement and stepped out into the bright daylight, covering their eyes.

"Those guards could be watching us right now, boss," Fletcher whispered.

"Then they should be worried," Gladius retorted as he donned his helmet.

They raced to their horses, leaping on them. They snapped their reins and sped off northwards, leaving the desolate town behind them.

The golden fields all around rustled in the wind as they scaled a large hill.

Gluttony's keep came into view far off. Black clouds swirled around the stone fort; the land surrounding it was a dead wasteland. They looked down to notice a trail.

"It looks like people were dragged to the keep," Fletcher concluded, staring thoughtfully at the marked trail.

"They'll see us coming a mile away. We have to walk through the crop-fields and sneak the rest of the way through that wasteland," Gladius delegated as they dismounted.

They left their loyal steeds concealed at the edge of crops and pushed their way past the tall grass.

A ragged scarecrow towered over them. Fletcher released a flurry of arrows, pelting the lifeless scarecrow.

"What was that for?" Gladius demanded. "You'll give us away!"

"Sorry, was just checking," Fletcher chuckled. The scarecrow hung ragged and broken, but lifeless.

Gladius shook his head with a long, drawn-out sigh.

"Well, that's where we need to be," he pointed at the scattered rubble in the wasteland. "It's been a while since I've had to infiltrate a town; I hope I haven't lost my touch," he sighed.

"Either way this demon has to pay for what it has done!" Gladius clenched his fist in determination as the two heroes disappeared into the tall labyrinth of the golden crop-field.

THIRTY SEVEN

FURTHER EAST IN RUMBLE Mountains, the slayer Robyn stood atop the cliff face overlooking The Lava Fields.

Her anger was still fuming, but after years of intense training by her mentor she had learned to channel it into a powerful weapon.

The swift breeze from the altitude blew swiftly by, her red hair flailed wildly in the wind. She contemplated her next move.

I'll need some help here, she realized, disgruntled at the prospect of asking for help.

There was a town to the north named Canyon Cove. Located in the Dry River Gorge, it was the home of her former teacher.

Once word circulated about Umbra she would surely rally support. Her old master, Cleo, a fellow slayer would surely help her.

She had made her decision and changed course north to Dry River Gorge. Her destination was Canyon Cove.

There is no way that necromancer can fend off two slayers! I'll have his head above my mantle in no time!

She strolled onto the trail heading north, and with renewed vigor she sprinted towards her destination. The weight of her weapons felt like nothing as her adrenaline pumped.

"You're mine, Umbra!" she growled.

Back in the squalor of The Wetlands, War Chief Groll marched impatiently through the camp his army had set up.

The many fires burned with the wooden bodies of the leshy that had confronted his army. Their damp bodies popped in the heat. Goblins and trolls crowded around them roasting anything they could find to eat.

The sounds of life in the surrounding area had been silenced, nothing but the roar of fires and deep voices of the soldiers was heard.

Groll snatched a boar shank from a nearby goblin. The goblin looked up fiercely, but shrunk back into his seat when his glare caught Groll's.

Groll strolled away taking greedy bites off the shank before tossing it casually over his shoulder.

The goblins and trolls munched their meat and chatted, the skeleton soldiers stood lifelessly on the outskirts of the camp as sentries.

The land around them emitted strange echoing noises; the rising sun shone fiercely at the destruction below. The wooded clearing was ravaged and bare.

A handful of goblins and trolls were still hacking down trees with their rusted axes and cheering gleefully as they fell.

"This place is so much fun to destroy," cackled one goblin. Their faces were lit up with delight when one of them suggested they burn the trees down.

They ran off to grab some lit tinder from the campfires, returning with blazing torches. One goblin who wasn't looking where he was going ran smack into the hulking body of a troll, dropping his torch into the muck.

The troll turned around. "You dare hit me?" he grunted. The goblin shook his head, insisting it was an accident, his fear evident. "Then I do this, little goblin," the troll smiled reaching down to pick up the torch.

The goblin stood frozen in fear wondering what the troll was up to. The troll swung at the goblin with the lit torch until he burst into flames.

"Eeeee!" the flaming goblin squealed, running around frantically.

The fire caught Groll's attention as he stomped towards the commotion.

The trolls and goblins stood around the distressed goblin laughing as he rolled around trying to put out the fire. Groll crouched down, gathering a hand of muck. He slung it at the goblin, smothering his entire body and dousing the fire.

"Enough of this foolishness!" Groll boomed. The laughing spectators stopped silent and dispersed.

Groll reached into the muck to extract the limp, burnt goblin. Shaking him wildly, he realized the goblin was dead and slung him into the undergrowth, watching him hit a tree and crumple limply to the ground.

"We march now!" he ordered. The camp fell silent and turned to him.

"Right now, Chief?" piped up one of the goblins nervously.

Groll glared at him, the goblin looked down. "Yessir," he muttered quietly.

Life returned to the frozen silence of the camp as they assembled their gear returning to formation. The skeletons assembled stiffly into their perfect square positions and awaited orders.

"Move out!" War Chief Groll demanded.

A hidden figure watched from the edge of the wilderness, letting out a sigh of relief that the invaders were leaving. "Parasites!" The figure growled.

THIRTY EIGHT

THE RUN FROM THE mountains to Canyon Cove was a short one. Robyn finally saw the town as she walked over the rising terrain.

The colossal canyon walls towered either side, casting a shadow over the town, darkening it more than midnight ever could. Small lights dotted the town from street oil-lamps.

Robyn marched into the darkened town. Her shadow danced from lamp to lamp. Her destination was the local tavern.

She wasn't going to drink, this was purely business.

The shaded wooden houses all around cast shadows on the street; the horizon was dominated by the rising cliffs of the canyon.

Robyn shoved past a local drunk who stumbled towards her. The drunk grabbed her by the waist and spun her around.

"How about a kiss, sweetheart?" the drunk slurred. He was incoherent of Robyn's deathly glare.

"No thanks, I'll pass," growled Robyn as she impaled him through his stomach with a sharpened blade. She leant over his shoulder. "That's not how you address a lady," she whispered, before extracting her dirk and walking away casually.

The man collapsed on the ground, bleeding out as Robyn strolled nonchalantly towards the bar.

An old wooden sign reading "The Rusted Nail" hung above the old tavern, illuminated by a dim lamp swaying gently. Robyn had not been here in a long time, yet she knew it well.

Robyn burst into the tavern. The joy and merriment froze as she scanned the tables. A crimson-robed man, tried to conceal his face from her, but she knew who he was immediately.

He noticed her as she loomed closer to him. Ditching his drink, he sped for the door.

Robyn tackled him to the ground just outside the pub and held a dagger to his throat. The silence was laced with fear as the gathering crowd stood quietly.

"Where is Cleo?" Robyn demanded, forcing the knife against the man's neck. She pulled back the hood to see a frightened young man staring back at her. His lips trembled, but he said nothing. "I'm not going to ask you again," she threatened.

"The slayer? He uh, gave me this robe you see. I uh, saved his life," he stuttered. Robyn's expression darkened as she exposed his lie.

Robyn knew he was lying. "Tell me now, or I'll gut you like a fish, boy," her anger raged. With one hand she corrected a streak of red hair that fell over her face. The man's neck dripped as she pushed the dagger closer.

"He should be back in town soon. I was uh, just borrowing his cloak you see. His house was empty when he left and I couldn't resist. Please don't kill me!" he begged.

Robyn returned her knife to her belt. The man let out a sigh. Robyn swung her fist and punched him right in his left eye, knocking him out. "Let that be a lesson to you!"

"Why don't you ease up on the boy there, he's only a harmless thief. He would have returned the cloak if you asked him."

"Cleo? How long have you been standing there?" Robyn inquired. She climbed to her feet and looked over to the edge of the crowd.

An older man clad in a mail shirt and leather clothes scratched his short beard. He held his other hand on the hilt of the sword that hung at his waist. His aged face and various scars all told their own story, he was an old pro and mentor to Robyn

"We have much to discuss," he said as he walked over to Robyn, placing his hand on her shoulder.

THIRTY NINE

BATTING THE STALKS ASIDE as he rustled through the field, Gladius' mind wondered to Marin. He had a sinking feeling about her.

Should I have let her go off alone with that necromancer?

He was beginning to regret his decision to allow her to travel to Sunrise City with Umbra.

"Is everything okay, boss?" Fletcher inquired, noticing the contemplative look on Gladius' face.

"I was worrying about Marin again," Gladius responded solemnly, his eyes staring blankly into the clouded sky.

"She'll be okay, Umbra seemed pretty reliable to me. And Astralode has that scrying orb, if she has any problems she can contact him," Fletcher reassured him.

It didn't work however, Gladius was still worried.

"Let's deal with this demon first," Gladius affirmed, storming onwards. Fletcher didn't pursue this conversation further and just followed him, saying nothing.

The two heroes finally reached the edge of the dying crop-field. Gluttony's fortress was on the far side of a decayed, dead plain. The peripheries of the fortress' grounds were clearly marked by the dead, grey vegetation it encompassed.

Luckily there was cover in the form of broken trade carts, rubble, and piles of dusty bones. The two heroes took a moment to gather themselves before they darted to the nearest broken cart. A skeleton sat, crumpled at the helm, the reins severed. The horses were long gone, presumably the lucky escapees from the nightmarish wasteland.

They crouched behind the fallen cart and looked up at the fortress' high walls.

Strange creatures patrolled the walls. They were hunched, grey creatures, with small heads and curved tusks. Gladius and Fletcher had never seen such creatures before.

"They look like summoned creatures, they seem so unnatural," Gladius recalled Seth's familiars from the siege years back.

The twisted figures lacked any consistency in their design, almost like they were just thrown together, they were true abominations. These creatures and their warped design now reminded him of the necromancer Seth's minions.

Gladius slid on his helm, concealing clenched teeth as he replayed the events all those years back when he battled that fiend, Seth.

The most disturbing part was how he had the same cold, disconnected presence that Umbra had, like a detachment from moral obligation. Umbra had proven himself otherwise by defending Myst City from the vampires, but because of his resemblance to Seth Gladius couldn't trust him entirely.

"So how do we get inside?" Fletcher inquired jerking Gladius out of his deep contemplation. They looked up to the guards walking awkwardly across the walls.

FOURTY

THE PUB LIGHTS FLICKERED, a thunder storm erupted outside The Rusted Nail, the rain crashed down washing out the cobble streets. The other patrons kept to themselves, ignoring the hushed conversation between the slayers, Cleo and Robyn.

"So you say you have found that necromancer, Seth's son? This is worrisome, if he's growing in power it won't be long until he turns and aids the demons," Cleo stroked his chin, a grim frown on his face.

"He is growing in power, I can assure you. He eluded me twice already and I fear I can no longer do this on my own. That's why I came here," Robyn grimaced as she swallowed her pride. It was very rare she admitted she needed help.

"He must be something special if the proud Robyn admits she needs help," Cleo commented as Robyn frowned at him. "Perhaps we could approach this in another way. You say he's traveling with a companion, we could use her to get to him," Cleo clasped his hands.

"How do you suppose we go about that?" Robyn inquired her interest growing.

A clumsy barmaid strolled nervously towards the table carrying a tray of empty glasses.

"Uh . . . can I get anything for you?" she inquired tensely, looking down at her shoes. She looked up to see Robyn glare, and quickly turned to leave.

"Okay, so here's what we do," Cleo stabbed a dagger into the table and leant on the hilt, edging closer to Robyn. "Have you ever heard of a leaching sphere?"

"It's a magical orb that drains magic. How do we find something like that?" Robyn inquired.

She was disappointed by Cleo's flawed plan. Her eyes widened when Cleo reached under the table and rummaged through his pockets.

"I've got it covered," he boasted, extracting a small black orb and placing it on the table.

Robyn brushed a strand of red hair from her face and stared at the orb intently for a moment.

"So how does it work?" she inquired with her gaze fixed on the orb.

"First you must lure him to use magic, then you block with this orb, once it's charged you can use it to drain that kid's magic power," Cleo explained. "I recommend we dispatch the girl beforehand, that way he won't hold anything back. She won't be able to heal him then." Cleo grinned revealing a blackened tooth.

"We should leave straight away," Robyn insisted.

The Contracted Soul

Umbra's heart raced as he dodged Pride's swings. Pride had discarded his sword and was swinging with his immense claws.

Umbra glanced over to Marin. She was twitching fiercely, the ogres around her were laughing maniacally.

The grim torches in the room flickered animating the shadows. The laughter echoing through the room was maddening, Umbra's head was spinning. With a loud thud Umbra was knocked onto his back by Pride's assault.

A line of blood trickled down Umbra's forehead. Umbra wiped it away with his hand. The purple symbols on his body were now raging, he grimaced from the pain. He felt like his body was burning up, his muscles were pulsing and tightening. It was like his body was being tugged out of shape.

A surge of strength flowed through him as he leapt to his feet; Pride had a keen look of satisfaction on his face. "Not much longer and you will be one of us," Pride boomed. The surrounding ogres cheered.

I have to get help for Marin! Umbra thought. He looked around desperately. Pride's glinting sword lay on the ground across the chamber.

FOURTY ONE

THE DARK STILLNESS OF The Dead Lands was disturbed by the shadowy steed speeding across it. The dust trail behind the horse swirled, the dotted skeletons and rubble were easily dodged by the phantom horse.

Micah and Vlad clung tightly to the dark steed. It was semi-transparent, and it was odd how they were able to ride something that looked like a shadow. The phantom horse made no sound as it moved, just the eerie flicker of dust flowed behind it.

"It shouldn't be much further, we're covering a lot of ground on this thing," Vlad called out loudly over the rushing wind.

"Now this demon, can she really help me become stronger than Umbra?" Micah questioned, his short blonde hair rustling in the wind. His hood flapped in Vlad's face, who was too frightened to protest.

"She does have limits to her power, but I'm sure she can help us. However, we have to be prepared to strike up a deal," he explained.

The phantom steed galloped onwards.

I know exactly what to offer her! Good-bye Vlad, you will soon outlive your usefulness to me. Micah grinned.

The monster that turned Lydia will be the key to avenging her!

The phantom horse leapt over a fallen boulder and clear into the air before landing perfectly on the other side without making a sound.

A massive storm-cloud gathered overhead as they neared Lust's temple. A light mist obscured their view as they galloped blindly onwards.

Vlad gasped as they entered the quickly thickening mist. The phantom steed suspiciously enough knew exactly where to go, unaffected by the low visibility.

Finally after a few minutes of blind riding the mist parted and a hulking temple came into view. Like everything else in this desolate wasteland it was a ruin.

Cracked stone columns and menacing stone figures of twisted beasts lined the walls. It was not what one would expect from a temple devoted to the demon, Lust.

The air was stale and heavy, it pulsed slowly as if alive. The door to this ruinous temple seemed to emanate an unnatural coldness.

The dusty wasteland seemed to stir to acknowledge the new visitors. As they neared the temple the hairs on the back of Micah's neck stood up straight, a cold shiver ran down his spine.

"We're here," Vlad whispered cryptically.

FOURTY TWO

THE JEERING CROWD AROUND Umbra was dizzying.

Hulking ogres pumped their hands in the air, cheering loudly. The colossal demon lord, Pride stood up straight and marched menacingly towards Umbra, who was panting loudly.

"I'm going to enjoy this," Pride chimed with an evil smile. He raised his curved sword and arched his back. He grunted loudly as he swung his immense sword at Umbra.

Umbra dodged clumsily to the side and clenched his fist launching a ball of dark energy. The energy struck Pride in his chest solidly almost knocked him off balance.

Marin was just a helpless spectator to what would be a fight to the death.

Umbra rolled to the side as Pride's next swing planted into the ground. He concentrated and his body began pulsing, a red aura surrounded him.

With a burst of speed he slammed into Pride with a tackle, once again merely knocking him off balance.

"Is that the best you can do, boy?" Pride chuckled as he regained his balance.

Umbra's scar lit up brightly as he continued swinging his fists at Pride. He attacked relentlessly, trying to spear him with his shadow. Nothing seemed to work.

Umbra's desperation was growing.

The sound of that jeering crowd is maddening!

Pride landed a punch right in Umbra's gut toppling him over.

"You know what you need to do to beat me," Pride grinned. "I sense immense power in you, boy. All you have to do is give in to it," he continued tempting Umbra relentlessly.

"Don't" Marin coughed weakly.

"Maybe you need more encouragement!" Pride grinned with his razor-sharp teeth. He turned to Marin and held up his hand in a choking motion. A shadow swirled around her neck and slowly tightened. She was lifted off the ground, her legs kicking frantically as she gasped for air.

"Umbra . . . no . . ." she wheezed painfully. Pride laughed loudly.

Umbra's anger was building, he couldn't contain it anymore.

The shadows in the room were drawn to him; they began to swirl fiercely in a tight circle. The purple markings appeared and lit up his body. His aura crackled a fierce purple and his eyes flickered white.

What choice do I have? He had to silence that foul abomination.

"Put her down now!" he yelled loudly, his voice deeper than before.

"Are you ready for a little game now?" Pride inquired dropping Marin to the floor.

Umbra looked over with his flickering white eyes at her limp body, returning his raging glare to Pride.

"No more games!" he growled. "You'll wish you never did that!" He lunged towards Pride, his body lit up in demonic symbols as his anger blazed.

Gladius and Fletcher watched from the shadows of the darkened courtyard in Gluttony's keep. They were startled by a loud scream.

"Nooo! You don't have to do this! Please!" a woman wailed hysterically. A group of grotesque guards dragged the rope-bound woman, passing in and out of the long shadows of the courtyard.

Much to their dismay, the two heroes recognized the woman immediately. It was that same woman they had found hiding in the village.

"We have to do something," Fletcher whispered, raising his taut bow. Gladius pushed it down.

"We can't give ourselves away," Gladius replied, averting Fletcher's attention to the numerous guards above where the lady was being taken.

The lady finally disappeared from sight as she was taken into the darkened tower. She had screamed herself hoarse and given up hope.

"We need to know what we're dealing with here. Gluttony is a demon lord so we can't take him lightly," Fletcher insisted, his gaze fixed on the guards.

"We'll contact Astralode with the scrying orb and ask him," Gladius extracted the small, crystal ball from a sachet at his waist.

He held it in front of him and concentrated. "Astralode, we need your help, can you hear me?" he spoke into the orb.

FOURTY THREE

ASTRALODE MARCHED DOWN THE lavish marble chambers towards the king's throne room. His cloak dragged behind him on the floor, in his haste he didn't notice. His mind was burdened with important information.

He approached the tall arches of the doorway. The royal guards uncrossed their pikes and beckoned him in.

Their faces were barely visible under their loose-fitting helms. They were lavishly outfitted with shining armor and colorful tabards emblazoned with the symbol of Myst City—a lion with a crown and scepter.

With an exertion of strength Astralode pushed open the tall doors and stepped into the threshold.

Stain-glass windows illuminated the marble chamber. Vivid tapestries hung on the walls depicting the rich history and myths of Myst City. Stone busts of the former kings lined either side of the red carpet. The King sat on his ebony, jewel-clad throne, lost in deep thought.

"My liege," Astralode addressed the king.

The King slung his magisterial cape over his shoulder and sat up. His fine silk clothes gave off a sheen topped only by the crown nestled on his head. His troubled expression was evident.

The King must have a lot on his mind Astralode concluded.

"What can I do for you today, my loyal chronicler?" the king inquired warmly.

"My liege, I have news from Gladius," Astralode began. The King raised his eyebrows curiously.

"I hope it isn't another request to release a condemned criminal," he sighed, referring to Umbra's royal pardon.

"No, your majesty, Gladius and Fletcher have encountered a demon lord out west and are about to engage it in battle," Astralode explained as he bowed with respect, his beard hanging.

The king stood up and walked over to the nearest tapestry. The bright, intricately woven drapery depicted the Twilight Wars and the battle at The Great Fields. He hung his head. "I hope he knows what he's getting himself into. Those vile tyrants almost destroyed this land once. They've been a thorn in my side for too long," Without turning around he continued. "Which demon is he fighting?"

"Gluttony, one of the lesser," Astralode replied. The king sighed.

"Thankfully it isn't Greed or Pride, or gods forbid, Wrath," he sighed. "Those abominations are near invincible, and I can't afford to lose our best. Our list of allies grows thin, and our defenses were shattered after the vampires attacked," he mourned, running his fingers through his silvery beard.

"I have been contacted by Magister Lunaris of Darkwoods. He's pledging his loyalty to our cause in lieu of his debt to the Golden Sun," Astralode announced.

The king did not share his enthusiasm. "How do we know we can trust them?" he inquired sternly, turning to face Astralode.

"At this point we can't be picky with our few allies, we need all the help we can muster," the old wizard replied grimly.

FOURTY FOUR

PRIDE'S SWING TOOK UMBRA by surprise. Despite his size, Pride moved swiftly. Umbra was knocked back by a solid tackle into one of the cheering ogres.

"You get back in ring!" the ogre grunted, shoving him.

Pride stood with his arms crossed, a sinister smile across his dragon-like face. His cold, dead eyes met with Umbra's.

"The little lady here put up more of a fight than you. Isn't that right, my dear?" Pride motioned towards the now pale-as-snow Marin, hanging loosely in the arms of an ogre.

Umbra looked at her. *What choice do I have?* He clutched his hand, igniting his scar.

Sharpened spears emerged from his shadow and flew towards Pride, he dodged them effortlessly.

"Pathetic," taunted Pride. "Still not ready to fight for real?" he inquired devilishly. "That's fine, maybe you need more persuasion," he pointed at Marin and fired a thin red beam through her shoulder, she jerked violently, howling in pain.

"STOP IT!" Umbra boomed in an unfamiliar voice. He ran towards Pride, every step he took, the more visible the demonic runes on his body became. When he reached Pride he was crackling with energy.

Umbra's eyes faded to a deathly grey identical to a demon's. The pain of his wounds faded and his anger raged.

With one deft tackle he knocked Pride onto his back. Jumping to his feet, Pride grabbed him. The two were locked in a grapple, neither side yielding.

Umbra's now hulking muscles tensed and shook. Blood began to drip from Umbra's nose as he strained. With a terrifying roar he took hold of Pride's arm, tearing it off from the elbow.

The demon howled in agony, clutching his wound.

The dripping blood excited Umbra, he licked his lips.

What's happening to me?

He knew what he was doing was inhuman but he couldn't stop. He wanted to lick up every last drop of Pride's blood from the sandy floor.

Umbra glared at Pride, the demon lit up in a burst of purple flame, howling and shaking as the flames dissipated.

Before he could get up, Umbra was on top of him holding him by the throat. He squeezed until he heard the snap of Pride's neck, black blood sprayed him.

The ogres in the room fell silent as they saw their master die. Pride had an odd smile on his face, taking a deep breath he whispered to Umbra. "I'll see you in the pit soon enough,"

The demon's body quaked and shook, finally stiffening into solid stone, the twisted smile still frozen on his face.

The ogres fled for the door.

"Not so fast!" Umbra growled. The ogres burst into purple flames collapsing as charred skeletons.

Umbra looked down at his blood-soaked hands, horrified with himself.

He looked over to Marin. She was deathly pale, lying limply on the sandy ground. He rushed over to her, scooping her up in his arms.

He ran his fingers through her blonde hair. A tear dropped from his glassy eyes as they faded to normal.

Out of sheer impulse he scratched out a summoning circle around Marin in the sand.

"Contract demon! Show yourself!" he yelled at the top of his lungs.

FOURTY FIVE

WITHERED CLAWS OF WOOD reached painfully into the lightning-ridden sky. A greenish mist drifted eerily over the magma and stone below. Razor-sharp rocks jutted towards the sky calling out for blood while lava flowed through the winding veins fueling this craving.

This was the domain of Wrath, the greatest and deadliest of Zuul's generals and easily the most powerful of the demon lords.

Long ago this nightmarish hell-zone was a lush forest teeming with life; it had been a sacred forest honoring the gods.

Now the only evidence of any life was the marching path of Wrath's troops carved deep into the raw rock.

There stood the former Temple of Destiny, now known as the Temple of the Damned. The formerly proud, golden tribute to the divine was now a twisted black abomination depicting the macabre evil it contained. Carved monsters and skulls of the unfortunate covered the towering columns.

The roof was high enough to humble a man, but the vastness of this domain of evil would strike fear into his heart.

Wrath had seized control of the demon lords eons ago when their mistress was taken away. The loyal demon lords bowed to him, whereas the others rebelled or sought unbridled destruction.

Wrath sat atop his razor-sharp black throne peering into a dark scrying orb perched beside him.

He had been watching Umbra, and was pleased with the evil power now surfacing in him. Soon enough his plans will come to fruition, Zuul will be released and unify the demon lords once more. She would resume her campaign of destruction that she had started during the Twilight Wars.

For ages he had waited, watched, influenced and plotted: burning hamlets, enslaving races, wiping others out, and now he was close. His mistress and creator would return and unify the rebellious demon lords.

Those pitiful traitors!

Their divided strength was easily kept in check by the power of the cities of men. Only a unified front led by Zuul could overcome these kingdoms and bring Turbulus under control of the demon lords once more.

Zuul herself had unimaginable power. Once she was free from the underworld there was nothing that could stop them from exacting revenge on those who caged her in the pit like an animal.

Men, he hated those detestable beasts. How small, puny and ignorant they are. They hid in castles like cowards and attacked his brethren from afar.

Even their noblest soldiers were always willing to join Wrath's ranks for a false promise of power and immortality.

They call us demons a plague on the land, but men continue to sow more destruction, even against their own.

These once noble soldiers that joined him became living shades, lacking any compassion, mercy, or even free will. They were the perfect soldiers and additional men just continued to line up to join their ranks. Their withered hands and rusted weapons hung loosely from their hooded, ragged robes. They hovered silently in the night, never rest, or hunger; they desire only for death, they were the shadow-fiends.

The shadow-fiends were one of Wrath's greatest creations, once men, now monsters.

The desires of men are so easy to twist, their will so breakable.

Once their evil nature was cultivated they rapidly lost any shred of humanity, naturally falling into the ranks of Wrath's minions.

These eerie beings glided silently across the hellish lands of Wrath, not even stirring up the clinging green mist. They cut through the mist effortlessly as they paced the landscape. Without the need for rest they had patrolled endlessly for centuries.

Wrath sat patiently atop his throne, dreaming of the end of the world, eyeing the small glistening obsidian chess board perched on a nearby stool.

"Soon enough she will return, and on that day my reward will be infinite," he stirred restlessly, fidgeting with the dark board pieces.

The players were well on their way to fulfilling their roles perfectly. He needed only to find Pandora's Box and the key to Zuul's power.

A devilish smile lit up his demonic face.

EPILOGUE

BACK AT THE BONE-LITTERED chamber of Pride's camp Umbra stood impatiently, pacing past the demon-summoning array.

"Show yourself!" he demanded at the pitch of a yell. Marin lay lifeless at his feet.

The array finally lit up and a plume of smoke encircled the room like a shark circling its prey. After collecting and forming itself, it dissipated to reveal a familiar figure.

The hulking form of Belphagor stood there once more, arms crossed, towering over Umbra. His hulking body crackled with glowing embers.

"You again?" the demon chuckled, gazing directly into Umbra's eyes. "Here to make another deal with me?" the demon inquired casually.

"No games, no tricks. I want you to return Marin to life. I offer my soul to you right now, no waiting time, right now," Umbra stared intensely at the demon.

The demon raised an eyebrow and exhaled a wave of sulfurous breath. "Just your soul? You've already given me that. You have to offer something . . . more substantial," a devilish grin lit up his shadowed face.

Umbra swallowed hard, a bead of sweat ran down his cheek. "What else can I offer?" he inquired nervously. His time was running out.

"Offer me your mind, body and every fiber of your being. Or no deal, I'll just leave her to rot," the demon demanded, breathing heavily.

Umbra looked down at Marin after hearing the demon's ultimatum. She lay lifeless on the ground; the color of her face was a deathly grey.

He knew what he had to do.

"Then I want to know you haven't cheated me. I want to see with my own eyes that she's okay," Umbra declared, "then I'll hold up my end of the deal."

"Fine," the demon snorted, his eyes flashed red. He faded away in a wisp of smoke leaving echoing laughter in his wake.

Umbra let out a sigh. *What have I done?*

He had sacrificed himself to save the woman he loved. He looked down at Marin longingly. It had been a long time since he had been so selfless.

Marin stirred and rolled over as if waking from a deep sleep. The color had returned to her face, her life restored.

"Are you okay?" Umbra inquired softly. He offered his hand, helping her to her feet.

A tear rolled down his face.

A loving smile colored his expression as he looked longingly at Marin.

"Umbra, what's wrong? Why are you crying?" she inquired, embracing him tightly.

"Everything will be okay, Marin. I have given you the greatest gift—a second chance," Umbra whispered in her ear, drawing back with a solemn expression, tears glistening in his eyes.

Marin was stricken with concern. Something was terribly wrong, it was as plain as day.

"I died, didn't I?" she asked. Instead of answering, Umbra leant in and kissed her on her lips.

"I'll miss you," he whispered softly as Marin wiped a tear from his glossy eyes. His face was darkened with deep sadness.

His body faded, dissipating into the wind like dust in a breeze, every inch of him fading away.

Tears streamed down Marin's face when she realized what had transpired. It was just like the vision she saw inside Umbra's mind back at Astralode's library.

"Umbraaaaaa!" she wailed hysterically into the dead air, falling to her knees. She looked down at her finger to see the single beaded teardrop he had left behind.

To Be Continued in:

The Myst City Chronicles II: Twisted by Hate

The sun gradually retreated over the horizon as the villagers of Birchwood town strolled merrily around the market square while the merchants closed their stands. The straw roofs rustled in the wind as the mild breeze swept by.

Pierre, a young man and father of a small family strolled briskly to gather water from the town's well. He carried an old wooden bucket in his hand.

However, today he had an uneasy feeling as he neared the oil lantern that hung by the well. The market was empty now and the moon was peering over the horizon. The cold, damp feeling stiffened the hairs on the back of his neck.

Was this just a Chill? He wondered, attaching the bucket to the pulley system of the well. The feeling was still emanating as he wound the crank and lowered the bucket into the darkness below.

"Hmm, this is weird," he thought out loud. The water level was much lower today as he continually felt the tension in the crank. Finally, he was relieved when he heard a small splash. He cranked the bucket up slowly, feeling the weight of the water he had gathered. As the bucket came into view a sparkle flashed from the pale.

The creeping sensation was overwhelming now. It pulsed like heavy breathing, growing more intense as the bucket ascended closer.

Pierre hoisted the water-laden pail out and peered curiously into it. A peculiar dark object glinted from the bottom. As Pierre reached in to extract the dark object from the pail the intense cold, empty feeling was overwhelming.

It was a blackened, shiny box, small enough to fit in one's hand. Pierre looked it over curiously. All of a sudden the surrounding area went silent. No crickets chirping, no owls hooting, it was as silent as a tomb.

A sturdy lock kept the box sealed etched with a strange symbol. Pierre rolled the box around in his hand. In an entranced state he returned home with a blank expression leaving the pail behind.

He arrived home to the soothing sounds of his wife and young daughter snoozing peacefully. The crackling of the log fireplace sent out a soothing sound as it consumed the wood.

Pierre placed the curious, glinting box on the mantle-piece above the fireplace and turned to walk away.

"Freedom!" hissed a voice startling Pierre. The box once again emitted an un-nerving breath of cold dread. Pierre stared dumbfounded at the old relic.

Back in Wrath's tower, the Demon Lord stirred. Suddenly he was hit by a rush of realization and shot to his feet.

"Mistress!" Wrath exclaimed. He felt her presence a long way off.

She had returned.